SECOND CHANCES

Dominique wanted to look spectacular, and didn't question the reason why. The red silk gown she chose was sophisticated, elegant, and sensual.

Grabbing her tiny red satin handbag, she strolled out of the bedroom. Trent was in the living room. He must have heard her enter because he glanced toward the door while bringing a glass of iced tea toward his mouth. His mouth gapped.

Dominique finally admitted the real reason she wanted to look good. If the stunned look on Trent's face was any indication, she had outdone herself. He was slipping insidiously into her life, making her feel things she had promised herself never to feel again. She couldn't let that happen. She could handle friendship, she couldn't handle anything more.

Trent reluctantly admitted Dominique had a way of taking him further, faster than any woman ever had before. It was not a comforting thought.

The glass clinked as he set it on the coffee table and stood. "I'll apologize early for staring."

She smiled. "It's the dress."

Immediately his gaze swept back over the gown that covered from neck to knees but displayed the flawless perfection of the wearer. He swallowed.

"Shall we go? I don't want us to be too late."

Trent mumbled something, he wasn't sure what. Dominique could definitely be a problem.

BOOK YOUR PLACE ON OUR WEBSITE AND MAKE THE ARABESQUE ROMANCE CONNECTION!

We've created a customized website just for our very special Arabesque readers, where you can get the inside scoop on everything that's going on with Arabesque romance novels.

When you come online, you'll have the exciting opportunity to:

- View covers of upcoming books
- Read sample chapters
- Learn about our future publishing schedule (listed by publication month *and author*)
- Find out when your favorite authors will be visiting a city near you
- Search for and order backlist books from our online catalog
- Check out author bios and background information
- Send e-mail to your favorite authors
- Meet the Kensington staff online
- Join us in weekly chats with authors, readers and other guests
- Get writing guidelines
- AND MUCH MORE!

**Visit our website at
http://www.arabesquebooks.com**

BREAK EVERY RULE

Francis Ray

Pinnacle Books
Kensington Publishing Corp.

http://www.arabesquebooks.com

PINNACLE BOOKS are published by

Kensington Publishing Corp.
850 Third Avenue
New York, NY 10022

Pinnacle, the P logo and Arabesque, the Arabesque logo are
Reg. U.S. Pat. & TM Off.

First Printing: August, 1998
10 9 8 7 6 5 4 3 2

Printed in the United States of America

DEDICATION

Velma Lee Radford and Mc Radford Sr., rule breakers who loved unconditionally. I miss you still.

SPECIAL THANKS

William H. Ray and Ron Reagan for their photographic expertise and invaluable insight.

Ronaldo Cordova, President of Royal Choice Carriers, for his neverending patience and knowledge of the trucking industry.

Leo Wesley, a full blood American Indian and a citizen of the Muscogee Creek Indian Nation, and educator for the Dallas Public School for American Indian Studies.

Karen Thomas, for remembering a long ago promise.

Angela Washington-Blair and Carolyn Michelle Ray for always being there for me.

Bless and thank you all from the bottom of my heart. This book couldn't have been written without you.

Prologue

It was a night the elite of Houston society would never forget.

Felicia Falcon and Grace Taggart wouldn't have had it any other way. After all, over two hundred guests were invited to a black tie affair with the promise that something spectacular was going to happen. They had better deliver if they wanted to hold their heads up again.

The heavy vellum invitation stated quite clearly that the doors of the grand ballroom at the posh hotel where the affair was being held would close precisely at eight P.M., with no further admittance allowed. That the invitees were given only two weeks notice was nothing short of unheard of.

Not one single person declined. And those who didn't receive invitations tried to attach themselves to those who did. Here again, they were stymied—Invited Guests Only.

No exceptions.

The seating was carefully arranged so that guests of Felicia and Grace were kept apart. Speculations at the linen-draped tables flew fast and furious. Those who knew the stylish and elegant Felicia Falcon, a transplanted Bostonian, also knew that she and her husband had reconciled after a two-year separation.

Could they be repeating their vows, since they had eloped—much to the chagrin of her wealthy and influential parents?

On the other side of the lavishly appointed room, those who knew the down-to-earth native Texan Grace Taggart as a devoted wife and loving mother guessed the affair was to announce the engagement of her youngest child and only daughter, Madelyn. Grace's two older sons, Kane and Matt, were already happily married.

All of them were wrong.

The two black-jacketed waiters assigned to every five tables kept the guests plied with tasty tidbits and vintage wine as the clocked ticked closer to eight. At precisely eight P.M., exactly three minutes after the last hurried guests were seated, the swish of a pure white satin curtain on the far left of the immense room revealed thirty-seven elegantly attired people standing side-by-side.

Instantly, members of the Falcon and Taggart families were recognized. The faint whispers became more pronounced. With a lift of his large hand which held a fluted champagne glass, Bill Taggart, in a tailored black tuxedo, stepped forward.

The murmurs hushed as if a switch had been flipped.

"Ladies and gentlemen, it is with a great deal of pride and an equal amount of pleasure that I welcome and greet you tonight. Those standing beside me join me in thanking you for coming. Would you please stand with us as I make this toast?''

Chairs scraped the polished hardwood floor as people stood, their glasses already topped off by an efficient stream of additional waiters. When everyone was standing, glasses raised, Bill Taggart visibly swallowed, but his voice rang loud and sure and proud as he said, "Please join me in wishing health and happiness to Mr. and Mrs. Daniel Falcon.''

A gasp was completely obliterated by the swish of another white satin curtain in the center of the room. Standing on the balcony at the end of a spiral staircase were Daniel and Madelyn.

Daniel, his long, salt-and-pepper hair tied at the back of his neck, wore his tuxedo with the casual elegance of a man who is confident about who he is and his place in the world. Madelyn wore a showstopping, jeweled, hand-embroidered jacket over a full-length, gold satin gown with equal confidence and elegance.

The audience erupted into thunderous applause. The couple smiled joyously. As soon as the applause had died down and the forgotten toast was drunk, an unseen man stepped out and handed Daniel a cordless mike.

"Good evening, everyone. Thanks for sharing in this happy occasion with us. To those of you who know me, I'm sure this comes as quite a surprise. It did to me, as well.'' Daniel looked at Madelyn, who smiled bashfully at the knowing laughter of the audience. "Maybe that's why it's taken me so long to face the truth—that there is only one woman I'm ever going to love, and you're looking at her.''

The applause lasted for a full minute.

Madelyn leaned naturally, trustingly, against her husband. "Those of you who know me also know how stubborn I can be. Those of you who know Madelyn and her family know she doesn't take crap from any man, Daniel Falcon included."

More laughter and applause.

Daniel glanced at Grace and she nodded. "Madelyn is strong and independent, just as her parents and her brothers taught her to be. So it came as no surprise that shortly after we were secretly married almost five months ago that she showed the good sense to—I believe the phrase is, kick me to the curb."

"I don't mind telling you that I had to work hard to get her back. You'll never know my dismal feeling of utter despair when I thought I couldn't have her back in my life. Finding out she was carrying our first child made the pain all the more intense."

Although he paused, not a whisper could be heard in the room.

"I'm baring my soul tonight to publicly apologize to Madelyn, but also to let you know that she and our child mean everything to me. I'll do anything to make sure both are safe and happy." His piercing black eyes roamed over the room. Each person got the message: to harm the wife and child was to bring down the wrath of the father. No one doubted the retribution would be quick and merciless.

At Daniel's nod a waiter returned with a champagne flute. Daniel lifted the glass high and said, "Please join me in saluting my wife, Madelyn June Taggart-Falcon, a woman of extraordinary patience and a boundless capacity for love. I'll go to my grave thanking God for both."

Daniel took a sip of wine, then handed the glass to the

waiter. His arm securely around Madelyn's burgeoning waist at four-and-a-half months pregnant, he led her down the stairs to the sniffles and applause and whistles of the guests.

The moment their feet touched the gleaming ballroom floor, a waltz began to play. Folding doors moved aside to reveal a full string orchestra.

The guests continued to applaud as the couple twirled around the floor. The beautiful woman and handsome man—their eyes locked in eternal love.

Grace Taggart, in a periwinkle blue gown, clutched the hand of her husband and watched her daughter in the arms of the man she loved. She knew the mother and daughter relationship had changed and taken another direction, but that was as it should be. The main thing was that her daughter loved and was loved in return. Madelyn didn't need the formal wedding Grace had always wanted for her daughter.

She had Daniel.

Next to Grace, Felicia Falcon, elegant in a sky-blue Valentino gown, let the tears freely fall from her eyes. Her son was happy at last. She felt the callused hand of her husband on her bare arm and stared up into his jet black eyes. Thick black hair hung bone straight down his back and brushed across strong shoulders encased in the first tuxedo he had ever willingly worn.

How she loved this man—a man she'd almost lost because of foolish pride. Needing to be close to him, she leaned into John Henry's strong embrace, his arm pulling her close.

Daniel and Madelyn stopped and invited their guests to join them on the dance floor. Felicia watched as several young men in the extended Taggart family rushed toward their youngest child and only daughter, Dominique.

Dominique, exquisite in a sophisticated and flattering long-sleeved Mizrahi gown, put one red, manicured nail to her chin as if considering her choice of man. From beneath impossibly thick lashes she looked from one to the other, causing her long, lustrous black hair to skim over her shoulders and down her back.

Several other men joined the group. Her exotically beautiful face drew men like the proverbial moth to a flame. Only Dominique didn't let the men stay around long enough to feel the heat, let alone become singed or burned, Felicia thought.

Her daughter had inherited the best features from her Muscogee Indian father and African-American mother. Unfortunately, she had also inherited their stubbornness.

Dominique's laughter, low and husky, teased as much as her banter—about being unable to choose from so many handsome men, so she might just sit out the dance. Protests from the men rang loud and clear.

"After all these years she still hasn't healed," John Henry said softly to his wife.

"I'm afraid not. Worse, I'm not sure if she ever will, or how I can help her," Felicia admitted, her gaze on her daughter as she dazzled her admirers with ease.

"Do you think she will stay this time?" John Henry asked.

Felicia's hand tightened on her husband's. "If we're lucky. She seems serious about her photography, and wants to open her own studio. She's passionate about something for the first time in years."

"But not about a man?"

Felicia said nothing. The answer was obviously clear as Dominique chose the youngest person in the group, a boy of about sixteen, to be her dance partner. Felicia glanced at the disappointed faces of the men not chosen, nor would they be.

Daniel had found love. Dominique was still running.

Chapter One

"I do hope this is what you wanted," said Janice Yates, a thread of anxiety evident in her crisp Bostonian accent as she took the Second Avenue exit off Hawn Freeway in Dallas, Texas.

Sitting beside Janice in the vintage Mercedes, Dominique Falcon nodded, her pulse kicking up a notch. Her future might be riding on what she saw in the next few minutes. It could be the beginning of what she hoped was a career, or another disappointment. After facing five such disappointments in the past month, she wasn't looking forward to a sixth.

"We'll be there in two minutes," Janice told her, taking a left into Deep Ellum, an avant guarde art district near downtown. "The neighborhood is in transition from residential to commercial, so you have an eclectic mix."

"It's the studio that counts," Dominique said, hearing the doubt in her godmother's voice. In her search she had seen a wide range of photography studios from lavish to run-down, but it was the atmosphere for the work created within that counted, not the outer trappings.

"It's the building at the corner with the glass front and side."

Dominique, in a chocolate, double-breasted jacket, matching cuffed trousers, and long-sleeved silk bodysuit, eagerly scooted forward on the smooth, leather seat of the Mercedes. Automatically, her hand closed around the Nikon that was never far from her reach these days. She came out of the car as soon as Janice brought the vehicle to a parallel stop in front of the building.

Janice, stylish and slim in a fringed, glen plaid jacket and skirt, was almost as fast. She took exceptional care of her fifty-three-year-old body and liked to think she could still keep up with anyone half her age. She usually did.

Unlocking the clear glass door, she stepped back. "Stop staring from the outside and come on in."

With a smile, Dominique's long legs quickly closed the distance between them. But once she was at the entrance, her steps slowed. She wanted this to be the place.

Her right hand trailed along the S-shaped Plexiglas that separated the tiled entryway from the polished concrete flooring of the main part of the studio. Glancing back at her godmother, who looked as anxious as Dominique felt, she faced forward and stepped around the glass . . . and into her dream.

It was as if the room had been waiting for her, and she for it. She felt right. It felt right.

Sometimes it takes a little longer for some of us to find what we're looking for. The thought raced through Dominique's head. Her search had taken twenty-nine years.

Dominique slowly let her gaze roam over the enormous studio. White walls glistened. Immense, plate glass windows reaching thirty-feet high in front of her provided an unobstructed view of a small, well-tended park across the street that had a piece of modern art, three, black, wrought iron benches, and several small oak trees. Working in the studio would be almost like being outside.

One of the other properties she was shown had had a glass front, but had looked out onto a dreary office building. Perhaps because she was part Muscogee Indian, she liked space and the ability to see the faces Mother Nature painted on the landscape. Here, she could have both.

Overhead track lights were spaced every seven feet. In the far corner of the wall were bare rods waiting for canvasses and backgrounds. Next to them was a sliding steel door for deliveries. The setup was a photographer's dream.

"You're sure this place is for lease?" Dominique asked.

"I sure am," Janice said with a smile. "The man who was the previous tenant went to California with his wife after she was transferred there."

Dominique turned to the older woman, suspicion creeping in. "And you just happened to hear about it, when I've had realtors across Texas and the bordering states looking for a place exactly like this?"

"Don't you still believe in the power of a fairy godmother?" Janice asked, raising a finely arched brow.

Dominique laughed, a rich, throaty sound. "I believe you and my family would do anything to keep me close. Houston and Oklahoma are both less than an hour flight from here."

"Is that so bad?"

"No. I've missed all of you." She folded her arms. "But I need to know if Daniel or one of his associates owns the building. And if they do, please don't tell me the tenant lost his lease because of me."

"What a suspicious mind you have. As far as I know,

Daniel and the owner of this building have never met. I
knew you were looking for a place, and I put out the word
that if anyone heard of anything to let me know. I may
have lost some clout in the Boston community, but I have
contacts here." The hurt was unmistakable in Janice's
voice.

Instantly contrite, Dominique hugged Janice affectionately. Dominique hadn't meant to bring up bad memories.
Janice had been on a social and financial par with Dominique's mother until Janice's womanizing husband decided he wanted a younger wife four years ago. Greedy as
well as immoral, Wayne Yates started a smear campaign
about Janice's character that nearly devastated her.

When the messy and public divorce was over, her reputa-
tion was tarnished, the lavish home she had lovingly decor-
ated and cared for had been taken away from her, leaving
her bank balance pitifully low. She had left Boston, moving
first to New York and then finally to Dallas three years ago
to open an antique store.

"I know that," Dominique finally said. "But I also know
my family is skeptical about this newest goal of mine, and
with my track record they have every right to be. But I also
know they realize how much I want to succeed and will
do whatever they can to help me achieve what I set out to
do. I've let them help in the past, but this time I want to
do it on my own."

"So, do it," Janice said, the words a challenge.

Dominique searched the steady, brown gaze of her godmother for only a moment. Duplicity wasn't in Janice's
nature. She was too sensitive and too caring to be dishonest.

Joy and, yes, a tiny shred of fear, raced through Dominique. This was it. All she had to do was to be bold enough
to step out and take the challenge. If she were going to

make a name for herself in photography, she had the place to do it.

It meant moving, as she had so many times in the past, but this time she had a definite goal, a purpose in mind. That hadn't always been the case, she ruefully admitted as she gazed around the room.

Her wandering had initially begun as a means of getting away from the pain in her family's eyes every time they looked at her. By the time she had finally taken a good look at her life, eight years had passed. Eight wasted years.

Her delicate hands lifted and closed around the Nikon N90 hanging from her neck. Such a small object, but its power was irrefutable. With it, she felt powerful. Through the camera lens she saw what was, saw endless possibilities of what could be.

"I hope that smile means you're going to rent this studio and stay in Dallas with me."

Dominique turned toward the stylishly dressed woman a few feet behind her. "It's perfect. I couldn't have dreamed of better." She smiled down at her petite godmother. "All I need now are some clients."

"You'll have them once I start telling my friends here and in the surrounding Metroplex about you," Janice said with confidence.

A frown worked its way across Dominique's brow. "Remember, I'm Dominique *Everette.*"

Janice let out an exasperated sigh. "I don't know why you don't use your name. People would fall all over themselves to have Dominique Falcon do their portrait."

"That's exactly what I'm afraid of. You, of all people, know what I'm talking about," Dominique reminded her. "Mother was so worried about you when you left Boston. She would have done anything to help you. You accepted nothing but friendship." Dominique tilted her head to one side. "You didn't try to influence anyone with the Falcon name, either."

"I had something to prove," she said with a trace of bitterness in her voice.

"And you did. Janice's Antique Attic has done well." Dominique sighed. "Try to understand that I want to make it on my own merit, just as you did."

"In your case it's different. People would have probably cluttered up my shop not buying a thing, but they'll stand in line for the sister of Daniel Falcon and the daughter of Felicia Falcon to take their picture, and you know I'm right."

Dominique was unfazed. "Believe me, I've thought this through very carefully. I've been out of the country and my picture hasn't been in a fashion magazine for some time, so no one should recognize me. I've planned and budgeted. I have two years to turn a profit before the money I've allotted myself runs out."

"And that's another thing. I can't believe you want to pay me rent," Janice said testily.

"If I lived anywhere else I'd have to pay." Dominique refused to back down. "Don't fight me on this. I was looking forward to spending some time with you."

"All right, but I don't like it. The way you explained things last night, paying me rent leaves you with very little working capital to keep your business going."

Dominique's fingers tunneled though her thick black hair. "That's the way it has to be. Dominique Falcon may have access to unlimited capital, but Dominique Everette is an entrepreneur with a tight budget."

"I wish there was some way for you to show those fabulous wedding photographs of Daniel and Madelyn," Janice pointed out ruefully. "The way his hand was touching her face was almost erotic."

Dominique had felt the same way on seeing her brother and his bride in the forest glen she had created just for that shoot. It had been imperative that people believe the wedding had taken place much earlier than it had. She had achieved her goal and more.

Watching them, she had almost felt like a voyeur. After the session was finished, Daniel had stated he and his bride were going to stay a while and not to come looking for them.

Dominique could still remember Madelyn's shocked protest, and Daniel's answering laughter. Two hours later they had finally come home, looking disheveled and utterly happy until they spotted her. Madelyn blushed, but Daniel grinned like a rogue, picked up his wife and started up the stairs to their bedroom, whistling. She didn't see them until the next day.

It had been a fantastic picture because the subjects were amazingly photogenic, madly in love, and beautiful. All Dominique had to do was press the button. The camera, Daniel, and Madelyn did the rest. She knew that wouldn't always be the case. Yet, she eagerly wanted the chance to try.

"No, I'll do it on my own or not at all," Dominique said. "There is already enough speculation on the identity of the photographer. You're the only one outside the immediate family who knows I took those pictures, and it has to stay that way."

Janice made a face. "I suppose."

"I may not be able to show that picture, but I've an idea of another one that's going to be just as memorable."

"What?"

Dominique grinned. "Not what. Who? And the answer is you."

"Oh my," Janice said, her face glowing with obvious pleasure.

"Oh my is right. Let's go create some magic." Taking her godmother by the arm, Dominique started across the room.

After signing the contracts for a two-year lease which took a hefty chunk out of Dominique's budget, they dropped the film off at the photographic lab, then headed home. Dominique's spirits were higher than they had been in weeks.

Things were coming together. When she'd received Janice's call a week ago she had no idea she'd have a studio by the next Monday. Photographing her godmother had made her dream seem real and obtainable.

Janice parked in the detached garage of the one-level, ranch style home. Arm in arm the women walked beneath the ivy-covered breezeway leading to the back door of the kitchen.

Janice opened the door and they were greeted by the light scent of bayberry in the welcoming brightness of the spotless yellow and slate kitchen. Those colors were joined by mauve and hunter green as they passed through the spacious, antique-filled living room and continued down the hall on the way to the guest bedroom.

"If you don't like anything, we can change it," Janice said on opening the door.

"You have exquisite taste, Janice," Dominique said, already knowing she'd love the room. She wasn't disappointed.

The genteel elegance of the bedroom reminded her of an English garden. The walls were done in a dusty pink to compliment the soft floral print of the woven damask drapes tied back on either side of an upholstered Victorian window seat.

But the focal point was the elegant, eighteenth century mahogany bed with a shaped headboard and high posts with urn finials. The bed was lavish, with a matching comforter and mounds of decorative pillows that invited a person to lie down in luxury and comfort.

And everything looked new and fresh.

Dominique turned to her godmother. "What if I hadn't liked the studio?"

"I refused to let myself think you wouldn't," Janice said simply. "I'm behind you all the way in this."

"Thank you," Dominique said, giving the woman another hug. It felt good to have another person believe in her dream, to believe her vision could become a reality.

Although her parents and brothers loved her and were making the right overtures, they weren't completely sold on the idea that she wouldn't become bored and change her mind in a year or less, just as she had done in the past. Dominique's Place, a little bistro in New York, was just beginning to show a profit when she became restless and sold out in nine months. The Afrikan Art Gallery in Seattle only lasted seven and a half months.

She had been assisting some of the best photographers in Europe for the past two years, but this was the first time she was going to be on her own.

"I have faith in you. We all do," Janice said. "I'll go start dinner. Call your parents and Daniel, and meet me in the kitchen. We have some celebrating to do."

Setting her Louis Vuitton overnight bag on the bed, Dominique picked up the phone and called her parents in Oklahoma and her brother in Houston. Each one caught the excitement in her voice and wanted studio portraits done. Laughing, she had asked them to give her a little time.

Hanging up ten minutes later, she changed into white shorts and an off-the-shoulder knit top that skimmed a couple of inches above her navel. Humming, she headed for the kitchen.

The celebration dinner was a two-inch thick porterhouse grilled to perfection over charcoal, stuffed baked potato with the works, spinach salad, and butter pound cake topped with freshly made whipped cream and lush, ripe strawberries. Dominique teased Janice about making her fat, but she ate every bite.

Dominique had thought she'd miss the fresh vegetables and fruits she got daily from the Paris market. Janice was quick to point out that Dallas had its own Farmer's Market, and she shopped there at least twice a week.

Deciding they were too stuffed to tackle the kitchen, they had taken their glasses of chardonnay and gone outside to relax by the pool. The backyard was awash with flowering begonias and petunias.

Despite it being September, the temperature in Dallas still soared into the high double digits. Placing their drinks on the umbrella table that separated them, both women settled into chaise lounges several feet from the edge of the sparkling blue water.

"Evening, Ladies."

At the unexpected deep male voice, Dominique sprang upright and almost fell out of the lounge chair. Regaining her balance if not her dignity, she whipped off her sunglasses and jerked her head toward the sound.

Her gaze traveled up taut, muscular thighs encased in tight denim jeans, past a narrow waist, over an impressive chest to a sinfully handsome face sculpted in bronzed mahogany that an angel would have wept over. Her hand lifted and closed around thin air. She almost groaned over the loss. The photograph would have been sensational.

Unexpectedly, as she gazed into rich, chocolate brown eyes, she experienced the sense of being knocked off balance. Her hand clutched the edge of the chaise lounge. The irrefutable awareness annoyed her almost as much as her idiotic impulse to slip her shades back on to shield herself from his hot gaze, which prowled over her as if it had every right to do so.

The belated greeting that she had been about to utter died in her throat. She detested men who openly ogled her.

Her hard glare elicited a deepening smile that made her think of how a cat must look just before licking his chops and pouncing on his prey. As that thought raced through her mind an unfamiliar something stirred deep inside her. His impact on her senses was totally unexpected and totally unacceptable. She felt . . . restless.

In the past she'd had no trouble dismissing such ill-mannered men. Yet, this particular man with his deep, molasses voice flowing like a lazy, sun-kissed river and too handsome face made it difficult for her to do so.

"Hello, Trent," Janice greeted warmly. "You're off early today. It's only a little past seven."

He chuckled, a deep baritone sound that did strange things to Dominique's stomach. Maybe it was the second helping of pound cake overflowing with whipped cream and strawberries.

"Don't remind me," he answered, but his gaze never left Dominique.

Janice saw his attention on Dominique, frowned, and swung her legs over the side of the lounge chair. "Forgive me. Dominique Everette, Trent Masters—my friend and next door neighbor."

"Hello." His grin widening, he extended his hand.

Uncharacteristically, Dominique ignored the gesture. She didn't let herself think her refusal to take his hand was anything more than a firm rebuttal against his earlier rudeness. "Do you usually come over unannounced?"

The welcoming smile on Trent's handsome face froze. His outstretched hand dug in the front pocket of his tight jeans. Dominique considered the accomplishment a minor miracle. "It hasn't been a problem in the past."

"Trent has been a lifesaver to me since I've moved here, Dominique," Janice said, her gaze whipping back and forth between the two tense people.

Dominique caught the placating note in her godmother's voice and heeded it. If the man had helped her godmother, he must not be as rude and crude as he appeared. That didn't mean she wanted to be best buddies with him.

"If you'll excuse me, I have some things inside I need to take care of." She stood. "Good-bye, Mr. Masters." Her voice was cool and final.

Trent had never been in a blizzard, but he now had a pretty good idea how it must feel to step from the warm confines of the indoors into a blast of frigid air. Nonplussed, he watched the stunning woman brush by him as if he were the lowest kind of life form. Noting her head held high and her regal bearing, he had the irrational urge to either bow or laugh.

Looking at her sleek, golden brown body moving away from him, the wind whipping her wild mane of midnight-black hair as it skimmed the top of her swaying hips in the white shorts, another thought struck—how much he enjoyed eating chocolate swirl ice cream in a cone. Licking from the top to the bottom, then taking a good bite.

"Trent? Trent?"

Guilty, Trent brought his rampaging mind back, then turned toward Janice and took the seat Dominique had vacated. The canvas was still warm. It didn't take much imagination on his part to recall her utterly feminine and alluring body stretched out on the lounge and the turmoil it created within his own body or to imagine his fitted over hers.

"Not you too?" Janice almost groaned.

"What?" he asked.

Janice rolled her eyes. "Most men see Dominique and start acting as if they have a screw loose. I thought you had more sense."

Trent reached for the drink nearest him, sniffed, then put the glass back on the table. He needed something stronger than wine to fortify him. "So did I."

The older woman laughed. "At least you're honest about it."

"The drool on my chin would have probably given me away."

She smiled indulgently. "It's about time you started thinking about something else other than those trucks of yours."

"Just because I'm thinking doesn't mean I'm going to do anything about it." Trent shook his dark head and gave a long, telling sigh. "Women take too much time. Dominique more than most, I imagine."

Janice straightened her shoulders and sent him a stern look. "And why would you think that?"

"It obvious," Trent said, leaning back in the chair and crossing his long legs. "She has to know she's gorgeous, with a body to match. She probably could have any man she wanted. A man is going to have to put in a lot of overtime to keep her happy."

"I never thought I'd see the day you'd judge someone on appearance," Janice said ruefully.

Trent frowned, his gaze going back to the closed patio door Dominique had disappeared through. "Are you trying to tell me there aren't at least ten guys lined up to take her out?"

"As far as I know there's not one."

His frown deepened instead of clearing. "It's worse than I thought."

"What are you talking about?"

"Barracuda. Eat a man up and spits him out."

Janice surged to her feet. "If you say one more unkind word about my goddaughter, you'll find yourself unwelcome in my house or on my property."

He came to his feet as well. "Goddaughter. You've never mentioned a goddaughter."

"That didn't mean I didn't have one," Janice said. "She's opening a business in Deep Ellum, and will be living with me for an indefinite period of time, so I expect you to be courteous." Janice picked up the two glasses. "If not, you'll have to find someone else's pool to swim in and another place to eat." With that she swept into the house.

Dominique was in the kitchen washing up the dinner dishes. Setting the glasses on the blue tile countertop, Janice picked up a drying towel. "Despite that display of male stupidity, he's a nice, intelligent man."

Dominique clinked a china plate none too gently in the dishrack. "I hate being stared at as if I'm on display."

"I know. You may not believe this, but Trent seldom pays attention to women. It's kind of odd to see the turnabout. He's usually the object of female attention."

"Some women have no taste," Dominique said, trying hard to forget her own reaction to Trent. With her heart still thudding, it was impossible.

Putting the plate away, Janice reached for another. "On the contrary, Trent is considered a very good catch. He's in his mid-thirties, has a successful transport trucking business, he's handsome, and has a body that has been known to create a stir when he wears swim trunks."

Dominique didn't want to think of Trent in swim trunks. She was having enough trouble trying to forget his broad shoulders and the muscled hardness of his thighs in those disgraceful jeans. "He probably knows it and uses it to his advantage."

"Quite the opposite," Janice said, pausing between drying two forks. "He seldom dates. Says he's too busy running his business to socialize."

"With his attitude, who would have him?" Dominique asked, determined to dislike the man.

"Half the single women I know, that's who." Janice chuckled, then sobered. "If I know Trent, his conscience is already giving him a good talking to and he'll probably apologize the next time you see him."

"I hope that's in the year two thousand," Dominique said, snatching a wineglass from the counter.

Wearily Janice eyed Dominique's agitated motions. "If you cut your hand, you won't be able to use your camera."

Instantly, Dominique's hands stilled. "He made me so angry."

"Men were acting much worse at Daniel and Madelyn's reception, and they didn't faze you," Janice reminded her.

Head down, Dominique slowly began washing the glass. "I knew I didn't have to see them again. Masters is different," she explained.

"That he is, in many ways. I just hope you won't hold this afternoon against him, and will allow yourself to find out." Janice placed a hand on Dominique's rigid shoulder.

When Dominique looked at her, she continued speaking. "You both mean a lot to me, and I'd like you to be friends."

"Friends might be asking too much," Dominique said with a wry twist of her mouth. "How about we don't draw blood?"

"It's a start."

Not moving as Janice stalked away, Trent had winced on hearing the angry thud of the patio door closing. If she got the blasted thing off the track again he wasn't going to fix it.

Even as that thought came to him, he knew he'd do anything Janice asked him because of two things: he liked and respected her, and she had been right to ream him out about Dominique.

He wasn't surprised by how easily Dominique's name rolled off his lips. In his business you had to remember names. What did surprise him was his initial reaction. Hard and hot and stupid.

He shook his head ruefully. He was too old and he hoped too intelligent to act that way. He owed both women an apology, but watching the loosely woven patio curtains swoosh closed, he didn't think now was the time.

Looked as if he was on his own for dinner. He sniffed the air and recalled the smell of charcoal-cooked meat that had brought him over in the first place. Janice had probably cooked steaks on the grill he had spent all day setting up last summer while she stood under the protective covering he had built so she didn't have to cook in the sun.

With a last, longing look at the curtained door, he started home. Served him right.

But he couldn't help wondering how he was going to

face his meat loaf again. There wasn't enough sauce in the world to disguise the bland tasting concoction he'd stirred together two days before. Grimacing, he tried to remember if he had eaten the last of the warmed up chili Friday night.

Chapter Two

Trent was on his porch sipping coffee early the next morning when Dominique sprinted by, her long, sleek legs quickly taking her away from him. Today she wore a red and white nylon short set. A loosely woven braid as thick as his fist and as shiny and black as a raven's wing hung down her slim back.

Without breaking her measured stride she started up the sharp incline of the street. Her movements were graceful, effortless, and in perfect harmony.

He grunted. That was more than he could say for himself. He had had a restless night and this morning didn't seem to be any better.

He hadn't nicked himself shaving or stubbed his toe on the corner of his dresser in years. This morning he had been so preoccupied with thoughts about Dominique he had done both.

What was it about the woman that annoyed and excited

him at the same time? Whatever it was, he had better find the answer and quick. Friends, good friends like Janice, were too hard to come by.

Stepping off the porch, he dashed the bitter, three day old coffee into the grass. It was time to eat some humble pie.

He rapped once on Janice's kitchen back door.

"Come on in, Trent," Janice called.

Opening the half-glass door, he walked inside. Janice, her back to him, was at the stove stirring something. Eggs, he guessed. The rich smell of coffee and bacon had him salivating. "I'm sorry about yesterday."

Sliding the contents of the skillet into a plate, she picked up the slate blue stoneware and placed it on the table. "I knew you would be. Sit down and eat, since you missed your steak last night."

Trent thought longingly of the steak he could have eaten instead of the burnt chili he'd tried to reheat, then pulled out a caneback chair and reached for a fork. Eggs and crisp bacon filled the plate. He almost licked his lips.

His blessing was quick. The second he opened his eyes, he reached for a fluffy biscuit.

"Tsk, Tsk. If I didn't know any better, I'd think my cooking brought you over here this morning with your hat in your hand instead of decency."

He had the grace to flush. "I'd like to think it's more of the latter than the former, but you are the best cook in Texas."

"Humph," Janice said. Picking up his cup, she filled it with freshly brewed coffee. "You might be able to get by me with flattery, but Dominique is another matter. She'll try for my sake, but if you blow it the next time this might be the last of my cooking you're going to get for a while."

"If any man knows the value of a second chance, I do,"

Trent said with feeling. His life had always been that way—a series of events that at first looked bleak, then eventually worked in his favor.

Initially all he had understood growing up in the foster home was that his mother hadn't wanted him. It had taken years of counseling for him to see that perhaps leaving him warm, clean, and dry in a hospital bathroom was the best she could do for him.

The note—Keep him safe. I can't. Tell him I loved him, I did, but he won't remember—and a new, blue baby blanket were the only legacies his mother had left him. She had never been found. The authorities suspected she was in an abusive situation, and might have feared for his life.

The social worker and others had helped him realize that he could be bitter and angry, or he could take every opportunity that came his way and make a place for himself in a sometimes harsh, cruel world. It wasn't easy, but he had succeeded.

Janice pulled out a chair and sat down. "Believe it or not, Dominique is looking for her chance, too."

Trent stopped eating. It had struck him odd last evening and then now, that a caring, nurturing person like Janice had never mentioned a goddaughter she was obviously very fond of. "Is she in some kind of trouble?"

"No, and that's all I'm going to say."

He studied the stubborn set of Janice's chin and knew he wasn't going to get anything else out of her. His gut instinct warned him to leave it alone. He had his hands full running his business. He couldn't save the world. He'd tried.

He went back to eating his breakfast, but not with as much enjoyment. The thought of Dominique being in trouble was oddly disquieting.

                              * * *

Trent was waiting for Dominique when she returned thirty minutes later. Although he had tried, he hadn't been able to keep himself from trying to figure out what her story was, and why Janice had never mentioned her.

He was too up front and honest for secrets. But he respected people's privacy. And he readily admitted to himself that if Dominique didn't bother him in a purely masculine way he wouldn't have given the matter a second thought.

So basically the problem was his, not theirs. There was never a problem in life that he hadn't been able to work through, and he didn't see Dominique Everette as any different. He'd just wait until she finished her cooling down regimen. Then he'd go over, apologize, and get back to his peaceful life.

The first part of his plan was going smoothly until she started bending over, touching her toes. The red nylon shorts lifted and clung to her nicely rounded hips, and all his good intentions of ignoring his utterly sensual new neighbor slipped away.

Instead, he remembered one of the treats he liked best at the foster home was peppermint sticks at Christmas. Most of the other kids got tired of sucking on theirs and started biting.

Not Trent. He knew how to savor his all day long with long, slow licks. Up and down, up and down. Down one side, and then down the other. He had the best tongue twirl at the foster home.

A dog barked, drawing Trent out of his musing. Damn. He had done it again.

He was a better man than this. Women didn't faze him. He certainly didn't fantasize about them. He had normal sexual drives, but he controlled them, not the other way around. A man who couldn't control his sexual urges wasn't much of a man.

They certainly didn't get very far in the competitive business world. Especially if he had to build his business, the way Trent had.

Masters Trucking got him up in the morning and made him feel alive. He didn't have time for a woman. He needed to put a stop to whatever this was. His number one rule was his business had to be his number one priority.

Determined not to waste another moment, he strode down the steps and crossed Janice's yard. "Dominique."

She whirled around on the small porch. "Do you always sneak up on people?"

"Sorry. I wasn't aware that I walked that softly." His gaze didn't drop below her sweat-dampened face. He was actually proud of himself.

"If you'll excuse me." She turned toward the door and somehow he managed to step in front of her. Abruptly, she staggered back. "What are you doing?"

"Trying to apologize, and doing a poor job of it," he admitted ruefully. "Look," he said, running his hand over his close cropped hair. "I usually get along with everyone, but we seem to rub each other the wrong way."

Black eyes widened. Up went her cute little chin.

Trent thought, *Bad choice of words.* If they were ever rubbing each other, he was sure it would be the right way, and they wouldn't be having a problem. He cleared his throat and his mind of everything but getting his apology out before he messed up even more.

"I was out of line yesterday. It's not my practice to stare at women, even ones as beautiful as you."

"Now it's my fault for your bad manners," she said frostily.

"Will you stop twisting everything I say?"

She crossed her arms over her heaving breasts. "They're your words, not mine."

"Have it your way. I'm the lowest form of life for daring to look at you in anything but a respectful manner. You're a guest of Janice's, and her goddaughter. I value her friendship, and I wouldn't want to lose it."

"She's quite fond of you," Dominique admitted reluctantly.

"Something you apparently don't understand."

"I don't have to."

"That's where you're wrong," Trent said. "In case you've forgotten, Janice has few family members, and those friends who are close to her, she values highly. She won't like us being at odds."

Dominique glanced away. He might be rude, but he was also perceptive.

One of Janice's regrets about her failed marriage was that she didn't have any children. Felicia always maintained that Janice had left Boston because her ex-husband's new wife had a baby four months after their divorce was final, and three months after they married.

Janice had made her friends her family. She was generous and compassionate, and could always be counted on to help anyone in need, just as she had helped Dominique.

Trent continued, "All I'm asking for is a truce, for Janice's sake. We don't have to be best buddies or anything."

Dominique's head came around. His words were almost her own. She was in Janice's house, and as such she had to respect her hostesses' guest and friend, no matter how much he irritated her. Most of all, she knew he was right.

For reasons that completely escaped Dominique, Janice thought highly of the brash, insolent Trent Masters. Dominique didn't see why, but snubbing the man wasn't worth upsetting her godmother.

Her hand lifted.

Almost immediately his rough hand closed around hers. Heat like a sunburst splintered through her. It took all her control not to jerk her hand free of the firm but surprisingly gentle grip. "Truce. Now, if you will excuse me, Mr. Masters."

She started to brush by him. He moved again. This time she wasn't able to stop her forward momentum. The front of her body collided firmly with his. Breasts to thighs. Air hissed through her clenched teeth. She jumped back.

The look she sent him would have melted steel. "Mr. Masters, you're beginning to annoy me again."

"That's just the point. Janice is not going to believe everything is all right if you keep calling me Mr. Masters like you have a bad taste in your mouth," Trent pointed out, trying to forget the softness of her rounded breasts pressed against him or the silkiness of her skin.

Dominique conceded the point with a curt nod of her head.

"Is it me, or are you always this reticent?" he asked.

"I don't particularly like you."

"I gathered that, and I don't blame you. I admire honesty," he told her frankly. "I expect the same of myself. I was totally over the line yesterday, and if there's anything I can do to make up for it, I'm willing—except move to another planet."

She stared at his handsome face and silently wondered if the earnestness she saw reflected in his steady, brown eyes was real or part of a calculated act. Then she decided to give him enough rope to hang himself.

"All right. Trent. Now if you'll excuse me."

Trent watched Dominique close the door on him again.

His hand rubbed across his chest where he still felt the lush softness of her breasts. His heart rate was erratic, his breathing more so. He wondered if she felt the intense sexual pull, then dismissed the idea.

Despite what Janice had said, he was beginning to believe Dominique was a barracuda. Her only problem was probably a love affair that had ended badly. Trent suspected the man had gotten the worst of it. Dominique had kicked the unfortunate brother in the teeth and left him in shreds.

Shaking his head, Trent started back to his house. Of all the women to send his body into hyperdrive, he had to pick Miss Ice Princess of 1998.

No matter how hard Dominique scrubbed her body in the shower, the sensation of Trent's touch would not go away. No matter how much of her scented bath gel and soap she used, she still smelled his spicy cologne, and another scent that was uniquely his.

Throwing back her head, Dominique let the blast of warm water beat down on her upturned face. Of all the times for her body to remember its gender now was the worst, and with the worst kind of man.

Her only concern had to be with establishing herself as a portrait photographer, not with discouraging the unwanted advances of some Neanderthal.

She knew how to handle men like Trent—remain calm and cool, and above all never let them know they got to you. Dismissive without being cutting. The male ego was too big and too fragile to stand being rejected outright. If they stepped over the boundary as Trent had, then you cut them off at the knees. She should have looked down her nose at Trent, slipped her glasses back on, and acted as if he didn't exist.

Instead, her body had reacted to his before she had time to breathe. Eight years ago she had made a vow that her body would never rule her mind. The consequences were too painful. She had never broken that rule until now.

Straightening, she shut the water off and reached for a fluffy, rose-colored, bath towel. She could handle Trent, just as she had all the other men who wanted to take with no thought of giving.

She didn't dare let herself think of the consequences if she could not.

"I can't believe this," Janice said, twisting the ignition key again and getting even less results. This time the motor turned over only once. Another switch of the ignition key elicited nothing. "I can't believe this. You're going to miss your plane."

"I'll call a cab," Dominique said. At any other time she would have taken a later flight, but she was anxious to leave. She refused to think Trent might be the reason. She had never run from a man in her life, and she didn't intend to start.

Janice shook her cap of dark curls. "This isn't a usual cab route. It'll take forever." Pulling her cell phone out of her oversized Gucci bag, she punched in a number. "Trent, my car won't start and . . . thank you."

"He'll be right over," Janice said, deactivating the phone. "It's a good thing you had an early flight and we caught him before he left for work."

Dominique was going to reserve judgment. In a matter of seconds a metallic green truck with tinted windows pulled up behind them. By the time the driver's door opened, Janice was halfway to him. Dominique stared straight ahead and remained unmoved.

"It won't start," Janice told him again. "It was fine yesterday."

"Let me try." Long, muscled legs clad in sharply creased denim jeans preceded Trent into the sports car. Dominique's hands tightened around her purse. For some reason the air in the car seemed harder to draw in, the interior smaller.

Trent flicked the key. Nothing.

"It has to start. Dominique will miss her plane," Janice wailed, standing beside the open driver's door.

"You're leaving?"

The question sounded like an accusation. Dominique didn't want to face him, yet she found herself doing so. "Yes."

Hard, brown eyes impaled her. "I'm usually at the office more than I'm here."

It took a few moments for the implication of his words to sink in. He thought she was leaving because of him. On one hand, it irritated her that he thought he had that much power over her, on the other his statement showed he really cared for her godmother.

She responded to the latter. "I'm going home to pick up my things and then I'm returning."

For a long moment, their gazes clung. She couldn't look away nor did she want to.

Trent nodded once, emphatically. "You won't be sorry." Before she could answer he was out of the car and lifting the hood.

Dominique sagged against the leather seat and wondered if the ozone level was higher in Dallas than Houston. Something had to be wrong to make her act like a teenager with her first crush.

While she was trying to figure things out, her door opened. Trent stared down at her. "The battery is as dry as a sucked chicken bone. I'm not sure if I put a charge on it it'll hold. I'll have to take you to the airport."

"That won't—"

"Oh, thank you, Trent," Janice said, cutting Dominique off. "I'll call the auto club to come see about the car."

"I'll have Smitty come over, too," he said, then stared down at Dominique. "What time is your flight?"

"Nine-thirty," answered Janice. "Her case is in the trunk."

Trent glanced at the gold-and-silver-toned bracelet watch on his wrist. "Eight-fifteen. You still don't believe in giving yourself enough time, do you, Janice?"

The older woman looked chagrined. "It would have been fine if the car hadn't died."

Trent didn't comment, just looked back at Dominique. "If you want to make your flight we need to get going. It's a fifty minute drive without the morning rush hour."

She didn't move. "What about Janice?"

"I'll have someone come over."

Again he looked meaningfully at his watch. "I hate to rush you, but I have an early morning appointment myself."

She was a woman, not a child. "Then, as you said, we'd better get going."

Getting out of the car, she hugged Janice good-bye and went to Trent's truck and got in. She was a Falcon, she thought as she buckled her seat belt. Her female ancestors on both sides of her family were as brave and as resourceful as their male counterparts.

They'd needed to be. Ignorant and sadistic individuals saw the color of their skin and deemed African-American and American Indian women fair game to be used and abused. Despite tremendous odds, they had survived degra-dations and injustices no human should have to endure.

Her ancestors were princesses and medicine women, rulers and healers, fearless and daring. Not one would have given Trent a second thought.

Opening the door, Trent climbed inside and buckled his seatbelt. The roomy cab seemed to shrink. Tinted windows created a disturbing atmosphere of intimacy. She drew in a nervous breath and inhaled the faint, spicy scent of his cologne. For some insane reason she had the sudden urge to lick her lips. She groaned instead.

"You say something?" Trent asked as he backed out of the driveway.

"No," she said quickly, glad when seconds ticked by and he didn't say anything else. Something was definitely wrong with her. The only thing in her favor was that Trent didn't have a clue. Lord help her if he ever did.

Neither spoke until Trent passed through the ticket booth at Dallas-Ft. Worth International Airport. "Don't you think you had better tell me the airline, terminal, and gate?"

Dominique realized on hearing the question that she had forgotten to check the night before to make sure the gate hadn't changed. She gave him the airline, then checked her ticket to give him the other information he requested.

Trent moved over a lane and took the next exit. She was still gripping the envelope when Trent pulled into the parking lot on the upper level for departing flights. "You don't have to park," she told him hurriedly.

"Your flight leaves in ten minutes. I suggest we run instead of arguing." Grabbing her case out of the backseat, he took her arm and steered her across the street into the terminal.

The heat of his hand easily penetrated her light blue, linen jacket. She cut a glance sideways at him and saw the rigid profile of his face. He was just being courteous, nothing more. A few more minutes and she'd be on the plane.

The security buzzer sounded. She glanced back as a male security guard moved toward Trent. "Please try again, Sir."

"Go ahead, Dominique. I'll catch up with you," Trent said. He stepped through and the security buzzer sounded again. "Must be the keys."

"Beep again, Brother, and you're mine," said a statuesque female security guard a few feet from Dominique. Her dark eyes gleamed with interest as they traveled slowly over Trent's muscular body.

"I'll buy you lunch if you let me do him," stated another female security guard, her gold-tipped nails tapping restlessly against the metal detector in her hand.

The women looked at each other and burst out laughing.

"Dominique, go on," Trent told her again as he jammed his hand into his pocket and removed his keys, then tossed them into the waiting container the guard held.

Holding his hands up in the air, he walked through the security checkpoint again. Silence.

"Dog," said the first security guard who had spoken. "Did that brother have a body on him. I was looking forward to—"

"Come on," Trent said, retrieving his keys with one hand and reaching for Dominique with the other. His steps were hurried as he led her away from the disappointed security women. "Why didn't you go on?"

Telling him about the two woman ogling him would

inflate his probably already huge ego. "It would have been rude," she answered instead.

He grunted. "If you miss your plane, Janice is not going to be happy." He expertly steered her through the early morning crowd of business and vacation travelers.

Hearing the announcement for boarding for her flight, their pace increased. When they arrived at the check-in counter, only one customer service representative remained, and a long line of passengers waited to board.

"Seems I just made it," Dominique said, the huskiness of her voice more pronounced from rushing.

Before the words were halfway out of her mouth the agent abruptly lifted his head. Thin shoulders snapped to erectness. His professional smile warmed considerably as he greeted her, then went about checking her in.

Handing her a boarding pass he said, "I'm sorry, the other first class passengers have already boarded. It will be just a moment."

"That's all right. I'm just glad I didn't miss my plane."

"So am I," he said, his voice just shy of crossing the line between professionalism and flirtation.

Dominique felt a hand clamp on her arm and looked up at Trent. Her brows bunched. He was glaring at the too thin man. Not for one second did she think Trent was jealous. Rudeness just came naturally to him.

Freeing her arm, she walked to the window to wait to board. "Are you always like this?"

"What did I do now?"

"You looked at that poor man as if you wanted to take his head off."

"He deserved it."

"For what? Being nice to me?"

"For peeping down your blouse," he answered tightly.

"What?" Dominique exclaimed, glancing down. The

lacy cup of her blue bra peeked from between the opening of her unfastened buttons. She quickly redid them, then remembered the man's gaze dropping.

She flushed. "Thanks."

Trent's brown eyes rounded. "What did you say?"

"You heard me, and I'm not repeating it."

He smiled. "I guess I can live with that."

Her heart rate kicked up. He really did have a nice smile.

"Last call for passengers boarding Flight six seven six for Houston. Last call."

Dragging her gaze away she glanced toward the thinning passengers, then reached for her overnight bag. "I'd better get going."

Slowly, almost reluctantly, he handed her the luggage. Their fingertips brushed, and this time neither could deny the transfer of heat.

She moistened her dry lips. "Thanks for the ride."

"When are you coming back?" he asked, telling himself he was asking for Janice.

She bit her lip before answering. "I don't know, but I'll be busy when I do."

To Trent, she couldn't have said it any plainer. They might have a truce, but she still wanted to steer clear of him. He had never pushed himself on a woman, and he wasn't about to start.

"You don't believe in second chances, do you?" he said, then continued before she could answer. "As I said, I'm gone a great deal. Have a good flight." Tipping the brim of his Texas Rangers' baseball cap, he walked away.

Dominique watched him leave and felt oddly bereft.

"Miss Falcon, you'll have to board now."

Dominique jerked her head around to see the ticket agent. "Thank you," she said coolly. The smile on his narrow face turned to puzzlement as she brushed past him and headed for the gate.

She didn't look back.

If she had she would have seen Trent stop and turn around. He stayed there until the gate closed and the airplane taxied down the runway.

Dominique wasn't as cold as he had thought, but the realization didn't make him any happier. Apparently neither one of them was looking for an affair, yet the attraction between them was getting stronger each time they were together.

So there was only one thing to do. Keep the hell away from her and pray she did the same with him.

Chapter Three

As soon as the flight attendant gave the clearance to make in-flight calls, Dominique dialed Janice's home number. She was mildly surprised when her godmother answered the phone. Trent's assessment was correct, she informed Dominique. His mechanic, Smitty, had brought a battery and installed it for her.

Trent always took care of her. He was such a fine, conscientious man, she said. You didn't find too many young people who were concerned with older people, especially if they weren't related to them.

Dominique didn't want to hear about the sterling qualities of a man who confused, irritated, and excited her in equal measure, but Janice was on a roll. Dominique mumbled the appropriate words politely when it was time for an answer, but as soon as Janice started winding down Dominique told her godmother she'd call that night.

Replacing the receiver, she sat back in her seat and tried

to think of anything but intense brown eyes that could melt stone and make her body tremble.

"Excuse me, Miss. I know this must sound like a line, but don't I know you?"

He didn't, but that didn't keep the suave and polished business executive sitting next to her from trying to pick her up. She resorted to her old standby of pleading a headache, putting on her shades, and turning her shoulder to him during the rest of the flight.

The second the FASTEN SEAT BELT sign blinked off after landing forty-eight long minutes later in Houston, Dominique pushed her glasses atop her head, stood, and reached for her bag. Her seatmate, the two men across the aisle, and the male flight attendant hurried to help her. Restraining herself from telling them that if they moved out of the way she could do it better and faster, she kept a smile plastered on her face.

Overnighter in hand, she left the airplane at a brisk pace. The business executive sprinted to catch up with her. Unfortunately, Dominique was beginning to develop a real headache.

Her gaze was glacial. "I don't know any more ways to indicate I'm not interested, and I don't intend to try. Good-bye."

Gripping her luggage, she started out of the portable boarding tunnel. The other two men who had tried to help her with her bag hurried by.

She spotted Higgins—now her mother's chauffeur, and her grandparents' before that—as soon as she came out of the tunnel. Despite his seventy-two years his shoulders were straight beneath his tailored, two-button pinstripe navy suit. The gray abstract tie was silk, the shoes Bally.

She smiled warmly. More than one man watched enviously as she hugged the elderly man.

"Hello, Higgins. I was afraid you might forget me since you have so much time on your hands now," she teased.

"Shame on you, Dominique, for saying such a thing," he greeted, reaching for her case. He might be formal with the rest of the family when their guests or associates were around, but Dominique had always been Dominique. "When I talk to your mother again I'll have to tell her she still has work to do."

She hugged his frail arm, her steps slowed to match his. "You miss her a lot, don't you?"

He nodded. "But her place is with your father and I couldn't be happier. Besides, what would I do on a ranch?"

"I seem to remember Daddy had about five hundred head of cattle and a few fields that needed plowing," she chided affectionately.

Allowing her to go through the outside revolving door first, he followed. "I'm a city boy."

Dominique smiled, secretly wondering if he knew her mother had said Higgins might have stood anything except the fact that the nearest store that stocked his favorite brand of Scotch was sixty miles away.

He would have stayed if her mother needed him, though. She hadn't. Felicia was no longer afraid to lean on her husband or share her innermost thoughts with him. She had finally progressed from an indulged young woman to a happy, contented adult, secure in the love of the only man she had ever loved.

After storing the luggage in the trunk of the shiny gray Mercedes, Higgins opened the passenger door for Dominique. Once she was settled he went around and got inside. "Have a nice stay with Ms. Yates?"

"Most of it," she said, then grimaced. She was not going to let Trent interfere with her happiness.

Higgins backed out of the parking space and merged

with the airport traffic. "I thought Daniel said you found a studio."

"I did. There were some other matters that I didn't expect," she told him evasively.

"Anything I can do to help?" he asked.

She sent him a warm smile. "No, but thanks. I have to do this by myself."

"I hope that doesn't mean you're going to go off again," he told her, stopping at a signal light. "It's been nice having you these weeks. I've hated to see you always leaving, and so did your family."

She took the slight reprimand with the affection behind it. "I hated it just as much, but something always pushed me to go."

"And now?"

She searched her heart, her mind. There wasn't quite the peace she wanted, but neither was the restlessness that usually haunted her. "This time I'm going to stay put. In Dallas."

He sent her a pleased look. "It's about time."

"Don't I know it," she agreed.

"You might even find a nice young man."

She stiffened. Not Higgins, too. Since Daniel had gotten married her mother had really been dropping hints for Dominique to find 'some nice young man.'

Dominique glanced at Higgins suspiciously. He and her mother were as thick as thieves. "I'm too busy for that."

"Nobody was busier than your brother, and look what happened to him," Higgins reminded her and took the on ramp to the freeway.

"That won't happen to me," she said emphatically.

The chauffeur shot her an indulgent look. "Seems I remember your brother thinking the same thing. I'd sure hate for you to go through what he went through."

"Could we talk about something else?" she asked.

"None is so blind as he who will not see."

"Higgins." She turned in her seat toward him. "What has gotten into you?"

"Nothing. Just remembering your brother, and remembering how much alike you two are." He sent her a sideways glance. "I'd like to see you just as happy."

She straightened. "I am happy."

"There's happy, and there's happy," he said cryptically. "If you want to know the difference ask your parents and Daniel."

Dominique leaned back against her seat. She didn't have to ask.

Her parents had spent two years estranged and hating every second of it, and neither she nor her brother had suspected they still loved each other and were miserable apart. Her hard-nosed brother seemed to have everything a man could want, yet she hadn't the slightest doubt his wife had given him a happiness that was clearly his greatest joy.

"Everyone wasn't meant to find that someone special," she told him. "Just look at you."

"I do every morning when I shave, and every night when I pass the mirror on the dresser and climb into an empty bed. There's no one there staring back at me except me. Once it didn't matter," he told her. "Seeing the excitement in Daniel and Madelyn as they get ready for that baby kind of makes me wish I hadn't been so finicky in my younger years. At my age a man sees his immortality and it's scary as hell. I don't want that for you."

"Higgins." She turned in her seat toward him. She couldn't think of anything else to say or do. She had always thought he was happy, his singleness something he had chosen. To think he now regretted the decision and was lonely was unsettling.

A frail hand reached over and patted hers affectionately a couple of times before returning to the steering wheel. "Don't fret. I've a good life, and the good Lord willing I've got some years left. Just promise me you won't look back on your life with a 'should have,' or an 'if only,' like I'm doing now. Live your life, go after your dreams, but remember dreams can't love you back. Promise me."

"Higgi—"

"Promise me."

"You know you're like family to us," she said, meaning every word. He was included in vacations and special events as one of the family, not as an employee.

He nodded his graying head. "I know. Sometimes I've thought of your mother as mine. She and I have been through a lot over the years." He sighed. "But there's a special bond between husband and wife, parent and child, that I can't transcend, that I'll never know. You can't tell me you haven't watched your brother and Madelyn and felt like an intruder."

She couldn't, but that didn't mean everyone would be as lucky. She ought to know. She had tried and failed miserably.

"Promise me," he urged.

"I promise to try."

He almost smiled. "You're as cagey as that brother of yours."

"Thanks for the compliment," she said, feeling more in control. She didn't need a man in her life, not now, not ever. So why did a picture of Trent Masters flash before her?

* * *

Trent couldn't concentrate. He'd tried. But a black-eyed temptress with long, black hair and a voluptuous body kept getting in the way.

Tossing the pen down on the bid he'd been trying to work on for the past two hours, Trent finally gave up. He'd bet dollars to donuts she wasn't thinking about him. She probably had every guy on the plane salivating.

Just as she had that ticket agent drooling. Trent got angry all over again. At himself and the agent.

He had noticed the man's gaze dropping and thought he was eyeing her breasts. It wasn't until after he turned her around to lead her away that he had seen the delicate blue lace as fragile as a spider web flirting with concealing her breasts.

Flirting, because the lace left the top swell deliciously bare. His blood had heated: his anger has risen.

He surged to his feet. He had promised Dominique they would be friends. Friends did not lust after each other.

The wooden chair creaked as he spun it around and plopped back down again. He was going to finish this report. No woman was going to interfere with his business.

The roar of a powerful diesel engine clearly came through the double office window. Trent lifted his head. The huge, black, seventy-foot eighteen wheeler with a two-foot-wide slash of red and yellow down the sides with Masters Trucking imprinted upon it slowly pulled into the complex.

Seeing one of his rigs never ceased to fill him with a sense of pride and accomplishment. There were forty-nine in all, scattered across the United States, Mexico, and Canada.

Pretty good for a man who had started out with a blanket and a note. But he never forgot things might have ended differently if people along the way hadn't helped him. Sure, people had tried to stick it to him—the woman he thought he loved for one—but somehow things had always worked out in his favor.

He had left West Memphis with the clothes on his back, a shattered dream, and a broken heart. On the way his new sports car had burst a water hose.

Randle Hodge, in a fifteen-year-old rig, admittedly stopped to harass the pretty boy in the sports car, but had taken pity on him instead. After jerry-rigging his hose, Randle had followed Trent to the nearest service station. Pulling a card that had seen better years out of his back pocket, he had handed it to Trent and told him to call him if he ever needed help.

Trent had tried to pay him. Randle had looked affronted and told him to just pass on the kindness if the opportunity ever presented itself.

In Dallas, Trent had found the job market slim. Needing money more than he did a fancy car, he had contacted Randle to see if he knew someplace reliable to sell the automobile. Randle had told him to come see him.

Randle hadn't been at home when Trent arrived, but his wife, Helen, had. After feeding him his first home-cooked meal in years, she had asked if he knew anything about bookkeeping. He should, he said—he had majored in finance in college.

Before he knew it Trent was living in the former bedroom of their oldest son and working as a sales rep, accountant, manager, and whatever else was needed for H&H Trucking Company. By the end of six months their profit margin had quadrupled.

On their first Christmas together they handed him a

large box. He had hardly been able to contain his emotions when he saw the toy truck with Masters Trucking on the side.

They said Masters sounded better than H&H. Besides, Randle had a greedy brother who would try to hit him up if he knew the company was turning a profit. Their children were all grown and had no interest in the trucking business. So, how about it? With the lump in his throat all Trent had been able to do was nod.

Trent had worked harder than ever. They had gone from one eighteen wheeler to two, and eventually to fifteen by the time the Hodges dissolved their partnership three years later.

Randle and Helen said they wanted to enjoy their money, and let Trent buy them out. He had hated to see them go, but wished them well. He had enjoyed talking over decisions with Randle, but as Randle had pointed out with a gap-toothed smile, all he ever did was listen, anyway.

That was ten years ago. Randle and Helen lived near Big Sur in a huge house that easily accommodated their six children and twenty-three grandchildren when they came to visit. They were a noisy, rowdy group when they got together. Trent was looking forward to spending Christmas with them, as he had every year since they first met.

As usual, Helen would ask if he had met a nice woman. Usually he had an answer—not this time. Picking up the pen, he went back to working on the report. It remained to be seen if Dominique was nice or not. The only thing he was sure of was that she played hell with his concentration.

Dominique was waiting at the bottom of the spiral staircase for Daniel and Madelyn when they stepped into the spacious foyer of their home. As usual she was struck by what a magnificent couple they made. Daniel, handsome as sin, in a charcoal gray, tailored suit that fit his muscular build flawlessly; Madelyn, her skin glowing and classically beautiful in a stylish, lavender maternity dress with a white collar.

Hand in hand, they smiled at each other with an expression that could only be characterized as pure bliss. Dominique's fingers closed on nothing. Her camera was in her bedroom. She sighed over the loss.

One thing was certain. Higgins had been right about that, at least. They did make her feel as if she were intruding on something uniquely private and profoundly special.

Daniel saw her first, his smile broadening. "Hi, Sis."

"Hello, Dominique," Madelyn said, moving closer to Daniel as he released her hand only to curve his arm around her thickening waist.

"Hello." Dominique came to her feet. "Daniel, if you have a moment there's something important I need to talk to you about."

"What's the matter?" he queried, a frown marring his handsome face.

Madelyn saw the serious expression on Dominique's face and eased away from her husband's loose embrace. "I'll go upstairs and change."

"That's not necessary, Madelyn," Dominique said. "I'd like you to stay."

Daniel sent his sister a pleased smile and pulled Madelyn back into his arms. She came easily, her head resting against his wide chest as if it instinctively knew it belonged there.

"Perhaps we should go into the study," Dominique suggested. "Madelyn, you've been at work all day."

Daniel's frowned deepened. "Maybe you should go upstairs and lie down."

"I'm fine." Madelyn patted her protruding abdomen. "Better if your son hadn't played kick all day."

He kissed her on the cheek. "I'll have a talk with him tonight."

Madelyn tucked her head and Dominique knew her brother was being playful and naughty—two things she had never known him to be with any of his women friends in the past. Turning, she went into Daniel's study, then closed the sliding doors behind them.

As soon as Daniel and Madelyn were seated on a small sofa, Dominique repeated her conversation with Higgins on the way from the airport and ended by saying, "I think he's feeling lonely and a bit left out."

"I distinctly remember him telling me he was too set in his ways for a woman," Daniel told her.

"That may be, but seeing your happiness and Mother and Daddy's has given him second thoughts. Especially when he goes home alone," Dominique explained.

Madelyn bit her lower lip. "I think Cleve sometimes felt the same way before Matt made him foreman of the ranch after Matt married Shannon. Just taking care of things around the ranchhouse and stables wasn't enough for his still agile mind, and somehow I think it made him think he was taking charity."

Distracted, Dominique ran a hand through her long, black hair. "I think Higgins feels the same way. A part of the family and yet separate."

"Well, it looks like we have to straighten him out." Daniel stood and dialed Higgins number. "Can you please come to the study? Yes, now."

"Daniel, what are you going to do?" Dominique asked.

"You'll find out," he said.

In a few minutes, Higgins knocked on the door. Receiving permission, he entered. His gaze leaped from one person to the next. "You wanted to see me, Daniel?"

"Yes. I need your help."

Higgins expression cleared. "You know I'll do anything I can."

"I knew I could count on you. The contractors start renovating the room next to ours for the nursery, and I'd like you to take charge to make sure things are done right," Daniel explained.

"I thought you wanted to take care of that personally," Higgins said.

Dominique's gaze went to her brother. So did everyone else. Daniel had interviewed representatives from five top architectural firms before making a final decision about which one to hire. No one doubted the newest little Falcon would be lavished with love and have the swankiest nursery possible.

Daniel looked straight into Higgins's eyes. "I could use some help."

"Please, Higgins. Maybe you can help Daniel remember moderation is good in all things," Madelyn suggested.

"I took out the sky dome, didn't I?" Daniel said matter-of-factly.

"Yes, and I love you for it." Madelyn turned to the elderly man. "You see. I need some help on this. That is, if you don't think it will be too much trouble?"

"No. Not at all," Higgins hastened to reassure her.

"You might as well move into the house. I want you nearby. That way we can discuss how things are going when I get home." Daniel hugged Madelyn. "Then, too, if Madelyn needs something and I'm not here, you'll be closer."

"All right." Higgins appeared dazed.

"You think you can move in tonight?" Daniel continued.

Dominique took the box and opened it. Inside was a heavy gold card holder for her desk and a monogrammed gold case which held a single vellum business card with Photographs by Dominique slanted at an angle in elegant script.

"As soon as you get your phone and the e-mail address Daniel says you have to have, you'll have a neverending supply," her father proudly told her.

"We thought it best if we had ours delivered," Daniel told her. "It's a complete computer set-up with your web site."

By the time her maternal grandparents had given her a beautiful leather portfolio with her single initial, and her paternal grandparents a Mont Blanc pen set and gold-leafed appointment book, her eyes were misty. "Thank you."

"You haven't received mine yet." Higgins handed her a gold bag from an exclusive gift shop.

Inside was a heavy lucite piece inscribed: "Follow your dream, but never forget your heart."

"Higgins, I didn't know you were such a romantic," said her maternal grandmother.

"A man must have some secrets," he said.

"One of them is how to get out of the sand trap," her maternal grandfather said. "How about coming back with us to Palm Springs for a little vacation? We could pair up and trounce Murphy and Thomas."

"I was hoping he'd come back with *me.*" Felicia took Higgins by the arm.

"Then you come over and we could finish our game of horseshoes," suggested John Henry's father.

"And stay for some of my famous pan bread," added John Henry's mother.

"Sorry, you'll all have to wait," Higgins told them. "I've

got to make sure the nursery is built right. Felicia, you have John Henry. And before you leave tomorrow, Edgar, I'll show you a sand trap secret or two. Mary and Leon, I'll be happy to visit when I've taken care of things here. Now, we should probably go in to dinner. Madelyn has been on her feet a long time." Reaching for the smiling young woman, Higgins led her slowly to the dining room.

Daniel shook his head, but he had a smile on his face. "I think I've created a monster."

"But you've made him happy," Felicia said warmly.

Dominique looked between her mother and brother. "You knew!"

"Suspected," Daniel confided. "You were the only one he shared his feelings with."

"Because he was worried about me," Dominique confessed. "But not everyone needs a significant other to be happy."

"Maybe not everyone, but I think Higgins is right. You weren't meant to live alone. One day some man is going to break through that wall you've built."

"I don't need a man."

"I didn't need a woman, but I can't imagine living my life without Madelyn," Daniel said with feeling. "Come on, let's go have dinner. I don't want to spoil tonight for you."

"You haven't. I know what I want out of life, and a man is not it."

Chapter Four

Camera in hand, Dominique bounded up the stairs to get another roll of film from her room. It was almost ten that evening, yet no one seemed inclined to call it a night. Daniel had tried. He had asked Madelyn if she was tired so many times that when he had done so again shortly before Dominique went upstairs, everyone in the room had answered in unison for her—"No."

With his usual self-assurance, Daniel had smiled and leaned back on the couch beside Madelyn. His arm around her shoulder, his fingers playing in her hair, he'd said, "Just checking."

Shaking her head at the memory, Dominique decided to call Janice as promised. There was no telling what time she'd finally come back upstairs. Sitting on the side of the bed she picked up the gold and white phone.

After the sixth ring, Dominique was concerned. After the tenth, she really began to worry. Janice hadn't mentioned going out. Absently, Dominique tapped the roll of film on her crossed knee. Where could Janice be?

She was about to hang up after the twelfth ring and redial when an out of breath male answered. "Hello."

Her grip on the receiver tightened. She'd recognize that deep molasses voice anywhere. And if her mind didn't, her body would.

"Hello," Trent repeated impatiently. "Look, whoever this is I'm standing here dripping wet from the shower, and I'm not in the mood to play games."

"What?" Dominique shouted, uncrossing her legs and jerking erect.

"Dominique?" Trent asked. "Dominique, is that you?"

"I wish to speak to Janice," she answered crisply.

"I hope you're not thinking what it sounds like you're thinking," he said, his voice taking on a stinging tone.

"Don't flatter yourself. Janice has better taste," she shot back, and meant every word. She didn't know the reason for his taking a shower in Janice's home, but she knew it was innocent. Janice didn't sneak around, nor was she two-faced.

Laughter flowed through the line. "You sure know how to keep a guy humble."

She hadn't expected the laughter or the strange flurry it created in her stomach. Restlessly she shifted on the handwoven bedspread. "I thought you said you weren't there very much."

"I'm not," came the reply. "I haven't been home ten minutes."

She frowned her confusion. "Home? I dialed Janice's number. I couldn't have misdialed. I don't even know your number."

"Janice had her calls forwarded over here. She had to meet an out of town client at her store," he explained.

Dominique cast the ornate clock on the bedside table a worried glance. "It's ten o'clock."

"The Nelson's could only make it tonight. They're good customers from Denton and she's met them at night before. Both teach at Texas Woman's University and can't make it until late."

"I still don't like it," Dominique said. She knew how defenseless a woman could be.

"Don't worry. The street her antique shop is on is filled with shops and restaurants, and well lit. Besides, the Nelsons always arrive first and always follow Janice to the freeway," Trent told her. "She has her cell phone, and if I hadn't thought it would be safe I would have gone with her."

Another thought struck Dominique. "If she had her cell phone, why didn't she just have her calls forwarded to it?"

"Because she gets so involved in phone conversations she doesn't watch where she's going." Dominique could hear the exasperation in his tone. "After two fender benders, the insurance company and I convinced her the phone should be used for emergency purposes only."

Dominique pulled her legs under her Indian style. "You do watch over her."

"I try."

"Thank you."

He chuckled, a deep sound that made her entire body tingle. She moistened her dry lips and wished he'd stop doing that. "Twice in one day. Something tells me I might be looking at some kind of record," he said, a note of amusement rolling through his voice.

She couldn't help the smile that formed on her face. "You might, at that."

"When are you coming back?" he asked, then added, "Janice told me to ask you."

"Thursday."

"Flying?"

"Driving."

"Start out early," he advised. "They're doing a lot of construction and the traffic getting in and out of Houston can be maddening. My truckers complain about it all the time."

"My brother, my father, and Higgins and I have already had this talk."

"Who's Higgins?"

"An old friend of the family," she answered, telling herself she wasn't pleased that he sounded jealous.

"How old is old?"

Dominique laughed. It just slipped out. He sounded so annoyed. "Seventy-two."

"You have a nice laugh."

Smiling, she slipped off her heels, scooted up against the headboard padded in silk brocade, then crossed her long legs. "So do you."

"Does most of your family live in Houston?" he asked.

"Just my brother. My father and his parents live in Oklahoma, my mother's parents in Boston," she explained, thinking of how they had all dropped everything to be with her tonight.

"You're lucky."

"Extremely. What about your family?"

"It's just me. I never knew my parents. I grew up in foster homes."

"Oh. I'm sorry." She felt an odd clutch in the region of her heart that he had had to grow up without the love and support of a family. She couldn't imagine where she would be without hers.

"Don't be. I've met a lot of good people through the years, and made some lifetime friends."

"Janice is one of them. She mentioned how successful you are. What you've accomplished is remarkable," Dominique returned, true admiration in her voice. She hoped she could do half as well.

"A lot of good people helped me along the way," he told her. "I don't want you to think I did it all on my own."

"Still, it must have been difficult."

"Sometimes, but I learned early that life wasn't going to give me anything. I've worked long and hard for what I have, and never regretted a moment of it," he said with feeling. "You can succeed just like I did."

"I'm going to give it my best shot," she said, her confidence soaring.

"Good. Hey, can you believe we've been talking for five minutes and neither one of us has gotten angry?"

"Maybe it's because we can't see each other," she said, and immediately a picture of him staring at her lips at the airport filled her mind. She got that restless feeling again.

"Maybe," he said, his voice oddly husky as if he were thinking of the same thing, "I'd better go. I'm getting goose bumps on my goose bumps."

She flushed and sat up in bed to swing her legs to the carpeted floor. "I'm sorry. I should have ended the call earlier."

"Don't be. If I hadn't wanted to talk to you, I would have ended the call myself."

"You're very frank."

"I've been told that, but then lies and secrets can destroy a person's life. I can't see a reason to lie."

While Dominique agreed with him in principal, she was harboring secrets of her own. "Sometimes extenuating circumstances demand bending the truth a little."

"Lying is lying no matter how you dress it up," came

the emphatic answer. Trent obviously didn't even believe in little white lies.

"I suppose."

"Glad you agree. I wouldn't want our friendship to suffer because we couldn't trust each other."

"You think we can be friends face-to-face?"

"The best. Good night, Dominique. I'll tell Janice you called."

"Goodnight." Dominique slowly hung up, fine tremors rippling through her, and it wasn't the prospect of opening her studio that caused the reaction.

"Trent Masters, you could be a real problem," she said. Silence was her only, unsettling answer.

In Dallas, Trent began whistling as he finished drying on the way to the bathroom. He wasn't aware that a broad smile accompanied the whistle until he passed the tri-fold mirror in his bedroom. He stopped, his gaze fastened on his reflection as if he was seeing it for the first time.

He didn't like what he saw.

"Oh, no you don't. Don't you even try to go there. Dominique and I are going to be friends. Nothing else." The second the last words left his mouth, he knew he was fooling himself.

Naked shoulders slumped. He had never lied to himself in the past, and he wasn't about to start. Dominique got to him on every level, and not just the obvious ones of her face and body. Her haughtiness challenged, her throaty voice intrigued.

What really got to him was that she needed a second chance—the one thing he believed every person deserved. How was a guy supposed to resist?

She was like no woman he had ever known. And she

was making him do things he had never done before. Not once in his life had he ever been jealous about a woman . . . until Dominique.

He had known her barely a day and he was ready to defend her honor and keep her safe. He could discount the airline clerk, but he couldn't discount that he had been jealous when Dominique mentioned the guy named Higgins.

He could still hear her sweet laughter, part teasing and part surprise. His body had hardened instantly. If she had been there, he would have pulled her into his arms and tasted the laughter on her lips, then the passion and need.

Trent spun away from the mirror. Jerking open a dresser drawer, he yanked out a pair of white cotton briefs and pulled them on. He then reached for a fresh pair of jeans. They were at a strategic point and going no further without discomfort when he glanced down.

His head lolled back and he stared up at the ceiling. *Why me, Lord?*

Dominique Everette could turn out to be a real problem and a test of everything he believed in.

Trent gave Janice five minutes to deactivate her alarm, grab a diet drink, and make it to her bedroom before he punched in her number. She answered on the second ring.

"Hello."

"Hi, Janice. Dominique called around ten. She's driving back Thursday."

"Thanks for taking the call," Janice said. "I thought you were coming for some strawberry shortcake."

Trent refused to glance down. "I'm not hungry."

"Could you repeat that?"

He knew Dominique could be trouble. Never in the past

had he had to think before he spoke. "I had something before I left work."

"Since when has that changed anything?" she asked.

He rubbed his throbbing temple. "Sometimes things happen when you least expect them."

"Trent, you know I'm very fond of you, but you're not making very much sense. You sound distracted. You and Dominique didn't have words, did you?"

"No. We're going to be friends."

"You don't sound too happy about it."

"I just have something on my mind tonight. Did the Nelsons buy anything?" he asked, grasping for a way to change the conversation.

"The Queen Anne secretary for Mrs. Nelson's office."

"Good. I'd better get some sleep," he said.

"It's only ten-thirty. Are you feeling all right?"

"I'm fine."

"Well, goodnight, and thanks again. I'll call her in the morning."

"Goodnight." Trent hung up and headed for the shower. Exercise sure hadn't helped.

Dominique's brow arched on seeing Daniel waiting for her in the dining room the next morning. A perfect, deep red rosebud lay on the pristine, white linen tablecloth by his coffee cup. She only needed one guess to know who the fresly picked flower was for. "Good morning."

"Good morning." Standing, he pulled out a chair for her, then retook his seat next to hers. "You seem surprised to see me."

She picked up her napkin and spread it on her lap. "As I said yesterday you have a lot on your mind, and I'm two years older since we had our last big brother little sister conversation before I left for Paris.''

His large hand brushed back a strand of heavy, black hair from her face. "No amount of years will ever make me stop worrying about you."

"You and life taught me to take care of myself, remember?" she said, spearing a cube of honeydew in her fruit cup.

"I remember a lot of things," he said softly. "The trouble is, so do you."

She couldn't deny his words. Her hand stilled, but thank goodness it didn't tremble when she turned to him. "I won't be made a fool of again," she told him, her eyes and voice as cold as ice.

"You're so much like I used to be it scares me." He held up his hand when she opened her mouth to speak. "I was so busy judging Madelyn on the basis of all the other lying, scheming women I had met, I didn't see her for the honest woman she is until it was almost too late. Be careful you don't do the same thing and let the past ruin your chance for happiness."

Despite her best effort an image of Trent crystalized in her mind. In rising irritation she firmly pushed the image away. "I'm happy for you and Madelyn, but a man in my life is the last thing I need."

He shook his head, his salt-and-pepper hair sliding over his broad shoulders. "As I said, you're just like me."

"Excuse me, Mr. Falcon, Mrs. Falcon's tray is ready," said a slim, young maid in a black and white uniform.

"Thank you." Standing, Daniel placed the rose on the tray, then took it from the servant.

"You'd better get that up to Madelyn," Dominique said, smiling that her guess had been right.

"Trying to get rid of me?" he asked, but he was smiling.

"No, but it's a thought. I like Madelyn," she said, leaning back in her chair. "She was all set to send her brother, Kane, and his family into the studio until I told her I wanted to keep a low profile."

"She's really big on family."

"Sounds just like the man she married. I've never seen you this happy."

"I didn't know I could be." His black eyes probed hers. "Don't let what happened eight years ago steal *your* chance for happiness."

Before she could speak he whirled and walked out of the room. *Just like Daniel to want the last word,* she thought. She watched him head toward the stairs, then she dug back into her fruit. Why was everyone so eager for her to have a man?

The answer came almost instantly. They loved her and wanted her to be happy. To them that meant a man in her life.

Before her disastrous marriage she had agreed with them. Now she knew better. The only thing that was going to make her happy was a successful photographic studio. Her mind firmly made up, she speared another cube of melon.

Finished with breakfast twenty minutes later, Dominique was rushing out the door when the maid informed her she had a telephone call from Janice Yates. Sprinting back, she picked up the phone in the living room. "Hi, Janice."

Janice didn't waste any time. She wanted to know every single detail about the surprise party. Dominique delighted in telling her. Teasingly, Janice told Dominique she had a present for her, but she had to wait until she came back to Dallas. Since Dominique loved surprises but hated to wait, she tried every way she knew to get the information out of her godmother. No luck.

"Stop fishing. My lips are sealed," Janice said, laughing, then sobered. "Trent phoned me last night to tell me you had called. He had sounded distracted, and he wasn't hungry."

Dominique barely kept from rolling her eyes. "Janice, Trent is a big boy and can take care of himself."

"I know, but he just didn't seem himself. Did you two have an argument or something?" Janice inquired.

"No we didn't. We were quite civil and mature." She glanced at her watch. "Gotta run. I have an appointment. See you tomorrow around eleven. Love you. Bye." Hanging up, Dominique shoved the thick strap of her oversized bag over her shoulder and headed for the front door.

Outside, she started down the curved stone steps just as the architect, Robert Lawrence, drove up. The short, compact man emerged from his metallic green Jeep carrying several cylindrical tubes beneath his jacketed arm, his movements slow and methodical.

When he saw her, his round face resigned, he tried to smile as he greeted her, but the results looked more like a grimace. He started up the steps.

Dominique said hello and got into her Jaguar convertible. She thought of telling the harassed looking man that Daniel had turned the project over to someone else, then decided to let him find out the good news for himself. Because no matter what Daniel said, he wanted nothing less than perfection for his first child.

Driving past the recessed double doors, she saw the architect being greeted by Daniel, Madelyn, and Higgins. Daniel had stayed to introduce Higgins. Madelyn had stayed to make sure Daniel didn't institute any last minute changes. Her grandparents remained in their rooms. Good thinking on their parts. The next five weeks were going to be very interesting in the Falcon household.

Her life in Dallas would be just as interesting. Downshifting, she pressed on the gas and zipped through the high, black, iron security gates of the estate. The red sports car gave her all the power and maneuverability she wanted. Although the vehicle was eleven-years-old, it had been meticulously cared for.

She hit the freeway with a burst of speed and merged with the traffic. Moments later an eighteen wheeler pulled beside her and tooted its horn. Her heart lurched. She glanced around sharply.

A bearded man wearing a once beige, straw cowboy hat grinned down at her. She waved and willed her heart to calm down. She was not disappointed, she told herself, but that day she spent an unprecedented amount of time glancing at the drivers of eighteen wheelers.

She also spent the day doing something else she had never had to do before—comparative price shopping. The owner of the third photographic equipment shop introduced her to price matching, turned his office over to her, and gave her a phone book, a pad and pencil, and a soft drink.

By early afternoon the trunk and backseat of her car were almost filled to capacity. She had purchased cameras, lenses, power packs, umbrella, soft boxes, stands, backgrounds, and the cases to store them. She couldn't remember ever having as much fun.

Pulling up in the circular driveway at Daniel's house, she got out of the car and went inside. Since she was leaving early the next morning there was no need to unpack the car. Heading for the stairs, her smile broadened. Her equipment took up so much room, she was going to have to take a small suitcase and ship the rest of her things.

"Miss Falcon, I'm glad you're here," said Mr. Lawrence, looking even more unhappy than he had that moring.

Her brow furrowed. "Is Daniel still here?"

"I wish he were. It's Higgins."

Her eyes widened in surprise. "Higgins?"

"Yes, Ma'am. Mr. Falcon said to follow his instructions, but I can't believe he wants to do something like this."

"Not the sky dome?" she asked, trying to keep a smile off her face.

The man's eyes widened for a fraction of a second, then shut.

"It was only a thought my brother had. Are my grandparents here?"

His eyes opened. Dominique couldn't figure out if he looked desperate or resigned. "No, they left shortly after I arrived and haven't returned."

Dominique's lips twitched. She'd always known the grands were intelligent people. "I'll go explain to Higgins."

The harassed man's appreciative gaze found hers. "Thank you. He's in the bedroom we're remodeling, watching every move my guys make."

"Higgins takes his responsibilities very seriously. My family has always relied heavily on him." She started up the stairs and the architect fell into step beside her.

"I heard you were leaving tomorrow with your grandparents. I don't suppose your trip can be postponed?" he asked hopefully.

"Sorry, I waited a lifetime for this. You're on your own."

His shoulders slumped. "I knew I should have been a dentist, the way my mother wanted me to be."

Dominique laughed, thinking she couldn't wait to call Daniel. He had never spoken truer words than when he said he had created a monster. Mr. Lawrence might not be happy, but Higgins would know he was loved and needed, and he wouldn't be lonely any more.

Out of nowhere came the questioning thought *When will I know the same thing?*

Dominique arrived at Janice's house shortly after noon, Thursday. Climbing from the low slung car, she stretched her hands over her head, then went around to the passenger side and got the one suitcase she'd managed to bring.

Janice, in a black gabardine coatdress with white collar and cuffs, met her at the kitchen door with a warm greeting and a hug. "You're an hour late."

"Traffic," she said succinctly, and set the small Louis Vuitton pullman down. "I have to be at the studio at twelve-thirty to let the telephone man in and receive some equipment I had to have shipped."

"What about lunch?" Janice asked.

"I'll grab a bite later," she said, and started back out the door.

"Here. Your present." Janice handed her a gold ring with three keys and the initial D. "The small one is for the glass storm door. The other two are for the double locks on the front and back doors."

Dominique clutched the keys in her hands. One more symbol that her dream was becoming a reality. "Thanks for this, and everything."

"You know you're more than welcome. As I told you, I'm going to enjoy having you here."

"I'm looking forward to living here, too." Dominique reached for the door. "I'm not sure when I'll be home."

"It had better be before dark," Janice said with a tinge of worry. "As I said, the area is in transition. It has a lot of traffic in the daytime, but things close up at night."

"Yes, Godmother."

Janice smiled. "Get on out of here. I have to get to the shop myself."

Smiling, Dominique hurried back outside and drove away. If she stared at Trent's house as she passed it was no one's concern but her own.

Everyone was late, and calling on her cell phone elicited little information. Worse, the electricity had not been turned on as promised, so there was no air-conditioning. She had long since plaited her hair, tied the pink silk top in a knot beneath her breasts and rolled up another two cuffs in her khaki walking shorts.

By five that afternoon she was hot, thirsty, and tired, and her temper was on a very fragile leash. Hearing the buzzer for admittance, she hit the control in her hand. Trent strolled in, looking cool and sinfully handsome in oatmeal linen slacks and a tan shirt, the long sleeves were rolled back to reveal the fine sprinkling of black hair on his arms.

Puzzlement drew her brows together. "What are you doing here?"

"Hello to you, too."

Irritated, she shoved a hand over her hair. "Sorry. This day has not been one of my best."

"Janice called and said you were still waiting on some service people and asked me to check on you," he explained. "My trucking company is a couple of miles from here."

"Thanks. I can't believe it's taken this long," she said, trying to keep her eyes from the white sack in his hand and not salivate at the smell of food coming from it.

"There's a tie-up on Hawn Freeway going in both directions, and one on Central Expressway as well," he explained, the sack still firmly in his hand.

"I hate to be gauche, but are you planning to share whatever's in that sack that smells so delicious?"

"Here," he said, handing her the bag and wondering if there might ever be a time when seeing her didn't hit him like a hard punch.

"Thanks," she said, hurriedly opening the bag. The aroma of fresh baked bread and spices wafted up to her.

Using one of her camera cases as a makeshift table, she placed the sack on top to use as a tablecloth and unwrapped her hot roast beef sandwich. Her mouth open, she glanced up to see Trent watching her intently. Her stomach did a predictable flip-flop.

She swallowed, then asked, "Do you want a bite?"

Yes, he thought *but not of the sandwich.* Gracefully, he came down on the other side of the case. "I've eaten."

She bit into the sandwich. The bread was soft; the beef juicy and delicious. She was aware of Trent watching her eat, but she was too hungry to bother worrying about it. Finished, she sat back and sipped on her drink.

"Missed breakfast, huh?" Trent said, his gaze running lightly over her mouth. The way she sometimes flicked her tongue out was driving him absolutely crazy.

"And lunch." She took another sip of her drink. The sweetened iced tea didn't help her dry throat. She wished he'd stop staring at her mouth. "I really appreciate your taking off work."

"I was closer than Janice," he explained easily.

For some reason his answer irritated her. "Thanks, anyway," she said, getting to her feet.

"You're welcome." He rose with her and walked farther into the interior of the studio. "Your studio has a lot of glass."

"That's what makes the place so great. It's like working outside."

He glanced over his shoulders. "I would have thought you were more the indoor type."

Her hand clutched the sack. "Somehow I think you mean the useless type."

"And what do you like to do outside?" he asked, ignoring her dig.

"Take long walks. Jog. Ride."

His gaze swept back over her before lifting to her face. "You certainly have the legs for it."

A spear of heat lanced through her. The door buzzer saved her from answering. She whirled away and went to pick up the automatic opener on her desk.

"Don't you think you should check before letting them in?" he asked.

She wanted to tell him to mind his own business, but anger was no reason to act irrational. She went to the door. "Yes."

"Telephone company."

She buzzed a tall, black man inside. After giving him instructions she turned to Trent. "Thank you for coming, and for the food."

"Trying to get rid of me?" he asked.

"Yes."

"Not a chance, Buttercup." Folding his arms over his wide chest, he leaned against the white beam separating the glass in front of the studio.

She was so startled by the nickname that she didn't say anything for a moment. "I beg your pardon?"

"Janice would skin me alive if I left you by yourself."

Janice again. "I'm a big girl."

His gaze intensified. "That's the problem."

Once again she felt the heat, this time more intensely.

"What kind of pictures do you plan to take?"

"Portraits mostly," she answered, her voice not quite steady.

"How long have you been in the business?"

"Not very long," she answered, unable to keep the worry out of her voice. Perhaps she should have given herself three years.

"Dallas has a healthy economy. You should do well." He unfolded his arms. "I might even break down and have you do a photograph of me, although I don't know who might want it."

"The usual recipients are friends, family, lovers," she said, knowing she was delicately probing.

He inclined his head toward the front. "An office supply truck just pulled up."

"Oh." Dominique went to answer the door, wishing the two men had waited a few minutes longer, then began chastising herself. She didn't want to know anything about Trent's personal life.

After that everyone seemed to come at once. She didn't have time to talk to Trent, but he was always there, a silent, disturbing, almost brooding presence. The workers obviously felt it, too, because they kept glancing in his direction.

It was after eight when she locked the front door. Darkness had descended. Janice was right. The area had a creepy, deserted quality at night.

A silent Trent walked her to her car parked parallel to the studio. He regarded the shiny, red Jaguar with a frown, then swung his gaze to her. "I thought you were just starting out."

She glanced from her car to the hard glint in Trent's eyes. "It's eleven years old, and the only car I've ever owned."

He didn't say it but the question was there in his expressive face, the narrow line of his mouth. How had she earned that kind of money?

"I paid for it myself with money I earned as a model in Europe, just out of high school," she told him, each word tightly controlled with simmering anger. She started to turn away, but his hand on her bare arm stopped her.

Intense heat radiated from his fingertips. He released her instantly, his hand balling into a fist. "You don't owe me an explanation."

"I wasn't giving you one. I was just stating a fact." This time she opened her door and got in. Tires spun as she sped away from the curb.

The hard blast of a horn from directly behind her had her gripping the steering wheel, but she slowed down, annoyed with herself that his opinion of her mattered, irritated that she had reacted so foolishly.

Trent meant nothing to her, she thought, totally ignoring the little voice that asked, *Then why are you so hurt?*

Chapter Five

Tires squealed. Trent was out of his truck and striding toward Dominique before her car engine died. His face hard, he jerked open her car door and glared down at her. "What the hell is the matter with you, driving like that?"

Calmly, Dominique picked up her purse from the seat and got out of the car. She angled her head back to meet his irate gaze. "I slowed down."

"Since when is seventy slowing down?" he snapped, wanting to shake her for being so reckless and scaring him half to death, disgusted with himself for making her angry in the first place. He had stepped way over the line. Somehow, though, instead of his apologizing as he knew he should, he let his temper get the best of him.

Midnight black eyes gave him glare for glare. "I was going sixty-five."

"Yeah, and zipping in and out of traffic like a jumping jack."

"You're exaggerating. I drive fast, but I'm competent." She pinned him with a look. "Since you arrived when I did, you must have been driving the same way."

He refused to back down. "How else was I going to keep up with you?"

Up went her delicate chin. "No one asked you to keep up with me. I told you, I'm a big gi—" She stopped abruptly.

His searing gaze lowered to her heaving breasts in the bright pink blouse. His hands clenched. He wanted to test their weight and resilience in his hand. Among other things.

A car passed. His gaze snapped up. Wide-eyed, she stared back at him.

He didn't blame her. His anger was displaced. He was totally out of line.

For the second time that night he had taken his anger out on her. "I know you won't believe me, but I'm usually a nice guy."

A satiny brow arched on her beautiful face. The wind tossed wisps of her black hair playfully. It was all he could do not to reach out, take it down, and run his hand through its thick, glossy length. "You've said that before," she reminded him.

"I know, and believe me I've never had to repeat myself in the past." He hesitated, trying to find a way out of his dilemma without compromising his principle about never lying, without admitting to his unreasonable jealously of the men watching her that had sparked his poor behavior. "You want to go get some ice cream?"

"No, thank you."

He hadn't thought it would be that easy. "Janice likes lemon custard. I'm sure if we went, she'd want some."

For a long time, Dominique studied his earnest expression. No one in her family was shy about speaking their mind, so his outburst hadn't bothered her. Considering what she had gone through eight years ago, her reaction surprised her. She hadn't cowered; she had faced him unflinchingly. It was as if on some basic level she instinctively trusted him not to harm her physically.

Another surprise. Rule Number Two: Give no man your trust until he's earned it several times over. Rule Number Three was also on shaky ground: Trust your first instinct.

"If that was an apology it's the sorriest one I've ever heard."

He tugged on the brim of his Negro League baseball cap. "Probably because I'm out of practice."

Up went that brow again.

"Now who's jumping to conclusions?" he asked. "The reason I'm out of practice is that I try hard not to put myself in the position of offering them."

The porch light clicked on. Janice stepped outside, her hand still holding the glass storm door. "Hello, you two. Dominique, I'm glad you're home. Everything get finished?"

Dominique turned. "Hello, Janice. Yes, thank you."

"Hi, Janice," Trent called. "I was trying to talk Dominique into going and getting some ice cream. You want your favorite?"

Janice's hand went to her slim hip in teal blue, wide-leg pants. "I probably shouldn't, but I can't resist. Go on, Dominique. You've had a trying day."

"I don't want it to become more trying," she muttered to herself.

"It won't."

She spun toward him. His hearing must be as acute as hers and her father's.

Trent met her inquiring gaze with that intense way he had of looking at her that left her restless and wanting something she didn't dare let herself think about. He was not a restful man to be around. "I don—"

"Please."

In her experience, a lot of men asked for a second chance, they even said *please,* but none made her stomach do flip-flops while doing so. At any other time, it would have been a clear signal to stay as far away from the man as possible.

With Trent living next door that wasn't going to be an option. Since she hadn't had these feeling in nine years, and never this strong, the best thing she could come up with was to stand her ground and hope familiarity bred disinterest.

"All right."

"Great." He grinned like a kid who had been granted a favorite treat. Taking her by the arm he led her back to his truck. "We'll be back in a little bit, Janice."

"Take your time. I have some paperwork to do," she said, then went inside.

Dominique climbed into the cab of the truck, wondering what she had gotten herself into. The door closed, and with it came the feeling of intimacy she'd experienced the first time she was with him in his truck.

The engine came on and she buckled her seat belt, wishing she could harness her erratic emotions as easily.

"Thank you for coming," he said, pulling off.

"Janice wanted some ice cream."

"I would have brought it back to her."

She turned toward him. "I know. Despite what's going on between us, you and Janice are genuinely fond of each other."

He stopped at a signal light. His gaze, searing and hot, found hers again. "What is going on between us?"

Her uneasiness on the topic clearly showed in her voice, "Perhaps you should answer that. You're the one who became angry this afternoon and tonight for no reason."

The light flashed to green. He pulled away. If he told her he was jealous of the men this afternoon, he'd be in more trouble than he was now.

"Well," she prompted.

"Those men annoyed me the way they were looking at you," he admitted, hoping he didn't have to be more specific.

"Me? They could hardly work for watching you," she told him. "You were like a dark, avenging angel waiting to dispense judgment and punishment on any person who displeased you."

Flicking on his signal light, he pulled into the parking lot of the ice cream shop, searching for a space. He had never been very good at hiding his thoughts. "It couldn't have been that bad."

"The phone company said the rewiring would take no longer than an hour. It took three. The cleaning crew promised to be out in two hours. They brought extra help because they were late, and it still took that long. Th—"

"You win," he said, holding up his hand as he parked. "You made your point."

"Good." Opening the door, she got out.

He met her at the front of the truck. His hand lightly touched her shoulder. "Wait." His hand fell to his side when she did as requested.

"You'll never know how sorry I am about what happened, especially the incident outside by your car. I have no excuse for such bad behavior." He stuck out his hand. "But if you can see your way clear to forgiving me and starting over again, I promise never to jump to conclusions again, and you'll never be sorry."

Dominique looked from Trent's steady hand to the steadfast gaze. His unspoken accusations had touched a hidden memory that had hurled her back into the past. She didn't like the journey, nor how vulnerable it had made her feel.

"Be very sure, Trent. You were right. I'm not much on giving second chances."

Neither his hand nor his gaze wavered. "I'm sure. We'll seal the promise with a double dip of chocolate pecan."

"Make it French vanilla and you have a deal." She lifted her hand.

"Deal." His callused hand closed securely around hers.

The line moved with quick efficiency. Before long, they were leaving the store with a hand-packed pint of Lemon Custard for Janice while eating their own double dip cones.

"Between you and Janice, I'm going to be fat," Dominique said, climbing into the truck.

"You have a long way to go." Trent slammed the door and got in.

"You want me to hold that?" Dominique asked, watching closely as Trent slid his tongue around the side of the cone. She felt funny again.

"Naw. After years of practice, I have this down pat." He proved as good as his word as he managed to fasten his seat belt, start the truck, and back out of the crowded parking lot with ease. "You're dripping."

"What?" She flushed.

"Your ice cream."

"Oh," she said, licking up the sides, feeling strange

sensations growing, gathering inside her like forces of energy.

"You have to have good tongue actions. You need more practice," he told her.

The force zipped like chain lightning through her, pooling in her lower body. She shifted on the smooth leather seat. *Girl, get a hold of yourself. He's talking about ice cream.*

"Here. Watch me," he said, and proceeded to slide his tongue expertly around the ice cream. "You have to go slow, so you won't miss a spot and drip."

She didn't want to think about dripping. Her teeth bit into the cone, relishing the coldness.

"Hey. You cheated."

She swallowed. "You didn't say anything about rules."

He glanced at her briefly, then centered his attention on the street. "I thought I did."

Dominique was grateful for the ice cream. It gave her a reason not to talk and something to cool her down. The moment the truck stopped in Janice's driveway, she was out the door. As before, Trent easily caught up with her.

"Do you always run wherever you go?"

"Sorry," she said, but she kept walking fast. At the front door, he held the hand-packed ice cream for Dominique while she unlocked the door, then gave it back to her.

"Goodnight," he said.

"You aren't coming in?"

"You've had a long day, and I promised not to make it any longer."

"You didn't." She smiled, meaning it. "Thanks for the ice cream."

"I still have to teach you how to eat it properly," he told her.

The urge to lick her lips was too strong for her to ignore. She didn't. She tasted vanilla, but it left her wanting. She

had a sudden craving to know how Chocolate Pecan tasted
. . . on Trent's lips.

"You missed a spot." The pad of his finger grazed across
the corner of her mouth and stayed there.

The strange feeling she had started having in the truck
crystallized into desire. It would be ridiculously easy and
so unthinkably foolish to turn her head and close her lips
over his finger.

"Thanks again." She averted her head and quickly went
inside. Leaning against the door, she closed her eyes and
tried to control the wild, pulsing need raging through her.

She hadn't had to deal with those emotions since her
divorce, since her life had turned into a nightmare. She
didn't want to deal with them now, but she didn't have a
choice. Trent wasn't going away, and she wasn't running
from another thing in her life.

She straightened. She had overcome problems in the
past. Trent should be no different. Even as she went in
search of Janice, she couldn't quite convince herself.

Head bowed, Trent placed both hands on the closed
door. Every muscle in his body tensed. His heart raced.
Desire pulsed through him.

He hadn't thought just touching her lip could make
every cell in his body quiver with need, hadn't thought
he'd see a matching need reflected in her midnight black
eyes.

What a mess!

Pushing away from the door, he walked slowly to his
truck, drove the short distance next door to his house,
and went inside. He didn't stop until he was stripped naked
and standing under the powerful blast of shower water.

If he didn't learn to control himself around Dominique, he'd have the highest water bill in Dallas.

Trent felt like a Peeping Tom, but that didn't stop him from watching Dominique through the sheer curtains in his living room as she passed by on her morning jog. It wasn't difficult to imagine her as a model. She was graceful and moved with a fluid elegance. He enjoyed watching her.

"That's not all you enjoy watching," he said aloud and dropped the curtain, aware he had done so because she had disappeared from sight.

He just didn't understand himself. Two weeks had passed since Dominique returned and he was still as hot and as bothered as ever. Each time he saw her he wanted her. Each time, the wanting was becoming harder to deny.

It wasn't as if he hadn't been around beautiful women before. Although Margo didn't have the unconscious sensuality of Dominique, she was gorgeous. And as dishonest as they came.

She'd had him so wrapped around her little finger that he hadn't known up from down. He had sent resumés all over the country in his senior year in college. His grades were good enough so that a few Fortune 500 companies were interested in him, but he had wanted to work in a midsized company where the advancement opportunity was greater.

Margo's father knew his daughter's charm, and had brought her along when he came to his university. Five minutes after Trent took her fragile hand in his, he would have done anything legal to please her.

He had taken the position of manager before even seeing the machinery company, and at less pay then he had been offered by other companies. He'd been caught by the entreaty in Margo's big, brown eyes and outrageously pleased that she thought he could bring her father's company out of its slump.

Once he was on board Margo had become more obvious with touches, low-cut dresses, the elusive scent of expensive perfume. She'd dangled her lush body in front of him as the prize while Trent put her father's company in the black again.

Fool that he was, he'd believed in her—his nose was "wide open." He worked like a dog—sixteen hour days, sometimes longer, seven days a week—until the manufacturing firm slowly turned a profit for one quarter, then another.

On one of those long nights he found out just what Margo and her dear father thought of him. Trent had been working late and had cut the lights off just to bask in what he had accomplished in ten short months. He was congratulating himself on how far he had come in twenty-one years. Soon he'd have a wife and family. He'd belong.

He had heard her laughter first. When he first heard it at the university he had thought the sound a bit shrill, but after falling in love with her, he thought it had a childlike quality.

The mention of his name had Trent sitting up and smiling, sure that they were going to say what a good job he had done and that Margo's father was finally going to give them permission to start planning their wedding, since the company was on solid ground.

He was wrong.

"Can you believe a nobody like Trent actually thinks I'm going to marry him?" Margo said, her voice scornful. "He could have insanity in his family."

"You've handled him very well, Margo," said her father.

"A few more months and we can get rid of him." He laughed. "He was so easy to manage. Thanks to you."

"I hope you remember what a sacrifice I'm making when the dividends come in at the end of the next quarter. There's a fabulous diamond bracelet and matching earrings I've been wanting."

"You'll have that, and more. Just keep playing him along."

The voices had faded after that. Trent had stayed in his dark office, angrier than he'd ever thought possible, until the night cleaning man had come in. Getting up, he had shoved all the papers on the desk in his briefcase and walked out.

He hadn't looked back.

Outside, he had stared at the ridiculously expensive sports car that he was struggling to pay for on his salary, one Margo insisted he drive—her future fiancé had an image to uphold.

Once back in his furnished apartment, he had looked around and knew there was nothing to keep him there. Packing his clothes, he had awakened his disgruntled manager to give her the key. His one stop was at the ATM machine, to draw out his $356.64.

He had taken the first interstate highway, then the next exit, and the next, stopping only for gas, until he ended up outside of Texarkana, Texas, with a busted water hose. Randle Hodge had come along, and once again, adversity had turned into opportunity.

Sighing, Trent released the past. He thought Margo had taught him to be wary of beautiful women who were financially unstable. He now steered clear of needy women like the plague.

He didn't mind lending a hand to anyone getting started, but that was all. He wasn't going to be used again by a greedy, unscrupulous woman, no matter how beautiful she was.

All that had been fine in theory until he had seen Dominique reclining on the lounger, heard her husky voice, watched the swing of her hips as she walked away from him. Lust, certainly, foolishness, most definitely, tested his rule each time he saw her.

Sipping the forgotten coffee, he headed to the kitchen and his breakfast. There was nothing worse than cold eggs, unless it was cold poached eggs. At least the coffee didn't taste so bad. Either that, or he had killed his taste buds.

He grimaced. He hoped not. His mind, like a treacherous boomerang, homed in on Dominique. He had gone to bed more than one night speculating about the taste of her lips.

Something deliciously sweet and maddeningly elusive, he imagined—like cotton candy, each taste always enticing him back for another taste, then another, yet never quite fulfilling the promise, always leaving him with the hope that the next time his lips closed over the sugary confection his hunger would be appeased.

He wouldn't mind coming back again and again, he was sure. The pleasure would be in the quest he would never want to end.

The ringing phone jerked him out of his musing. "Hello."

"Trent. We got a call from the electric company. They have a hot load of transformers that need to go to Ohio. A storm just blew through this morning. Who do you want to send?" asked the dispatcher, who then proceeded to tell him who was available.

"I'll take it," Trent said, dumping the egg in the garbage disposal.

Surprise registered in the woman's voice over the sound

of the running disposal. "You haven't made a run in over nine months."

"So, I'm long overdue." A few days away from Dominique might give him some perspective. "Be there in twenty. Have everything ready for me to pull out."

Hanging up, he rinsed the dishes, stacked them in the dishwasher, grabbed his keys with one hand and his baseball cap with the other.

In minutes he was speeding away.

Janice was speaking on the kitchen wall phone when Dominique returned from her jog. Opening the refrigerator, she poured herself a large glass of orange juice. After taking a sip she rolled the cool glass over her hot forehead.

"I'll take care of the mail and newspaper. Don't worry about anything. You just be careful. Good-bye," Janice said.

"Someone had to go out of town unexpectedly?" Dominique asked, sipping her juice again.

Janice bit her lip. "Trent."

"What's the matter?" Dominique asked, her heart lurching.

"He said he had to make a run with a hot load of transformers to Ohio," Janice explained, pulling her silk jacket over her leopard print blouse.

"He deals in stolen merchandise?" Dominique squeaked.

A smile took the lines of worry from Janice's face. "Hot in trucker language just means they should have been there days ago. Trent is honest, and has the highest integrity. I just wish I knew why he's taking off this way."

Dominique sat the glass on the counter. "You said he had to make a run."

"But he hasn't been on the road in months. I hope everything is all right."

"I'm sure it is." Dominique picked up Janice's purse and handed it to her. "Scoot. You have an eight o'clock appointment."

"Your breakfast is in the oven," Janice called, opening the back kitchen door.

"I told you I could fix my own."

"I enjoy cooking. You know that. I'll have to fix Trent something nice for his homecoming. Truck stop food ranges from excellent to awful."

"Janice. Will you stop worrying?"

"I'll try. It's just that he's been acting strange for the past few days." Coming back inside, she kissed Dominique on the cheek. "Have a wonderful day."

"I will," Dominique said, waving good-bye. Heading for the shower, she tried to run over the list of things she planned to do that day, but she couldn't put her god-mother's concern about Trent's behavior out of her mind.

Most of all, she couldn't help wondering if she had anything to do with his leaving.

Dominique's studio was perfect. The curved rosewood desk Daniel had included with the computer system was elegant and graceful. On its polished surface were the black Mont Blanc desk set, her appointment book, her engraved cards, and the lucite piece Higgins had given her. She had found just the right small couch and a table and chair within her budget for the previewing room, where she planned to show her proofs and slides to her clients.

If she ever got any.

Trying not to sigh, Dominique glanced around the studio. The only sounds were the gurgle of the water cooler and the soulful voice of Anita Baker on the CD player. Even the usually busy traffic seemed to have disappeared. Along with the potential customers.

She knew three weeks in business wasn't a long time, but she had thought she'd get some response from her radio ads on a popular R&B station or her web site. Well, she'd had some calls, but after she told people her prices they either tried to haggle with her or simply hung up.

Silver bracelets jingled on her arm as she picked up the slick brochure listing her prices, then leaned back in her leather chair. If she cut her prices, she wouldn't be able to meet expenses. If she didn't get some customers, she'd be out of business, anyway. This was where it got tough.

Either she could start second-guessing herself or figure out a way to get people into the studio. Her budget wouldn't allow for any more large expenditures after the radio ads.

She thought of her dynamic, stubborn family. Not one of them would hesitate to go down fighting for what they believed in. This time she was going to do the same. She set the brochure aside. Not one price was changing. That left her only one alternative—to develop a marketing plan that was inexpensive and effective.

Her front door buzzer rang. She spun around in her chair away from the computer and pressed the buzzer for the person to enter. In came a rather austere looking woman, elegantly dressed in a lilac designer suit, carrying a small white poodle covered with tiny, lilac-colored bows.

"Good evening. Welcome to Dominique's. Can I help you?"

"Yes, I'm Mrs. Hightower. Mrs. Harold Hightower. Janice mentioned you had just returned from Paris doing photography, and I want you to do Scarlet."

"Scarlet?"

"Scarlet," Mrs. Hightower repeated, lifting the dog.

Dominique didn't hesitate. Business was business. "Please have a seat and tell me if you have anything specific in mind."

Thirty minutes later Mrs. Hightower left, saying she'd call. Dominique doubted it. Her eyes had widened like saucers when she saw the price list. As the saying went, another one bit the dust.

The buzzer rang and she automatically glanced up. Her body tightened. Her heart rate increased. The sound came again, and she finally moved to deactivate the lock.

"Hi," Trent said, strolling in as if he hadn't been gone almost a week without a word. "I haven't been gone so long that you didn't recognize me, have I?"

"No, of course not." Did she appear as flustered as she sounded? Had the past five days passed so slowly because she had missed Trent, or because business was so slow? She didn't know and she wasn't looking too closely to find the answer.

Her hand swept over her hair and encountered the heavy silver and turquoise barrette at the base of her neck. The action was a sure sign of a woman primping for a man. Maybe she already knew the answer to why the past days had been so trying. "Hello, Trent."

He glanced around, noting the canvas and props. He wore a chambray shirt and the usual tight jeans that defined his long, muscular legs perfectly. "Looks good."

So do you, she almost said, and clamped her teeth together.

He turned back to her. "How's it going?"

"As well as can be expected," she said evasively. "How was your trip? Janice said you don't usually go on runs."

"I don't like getting rusty." He tugged the brim of his

black baseball cap with Masters Trucking in red block lettering on the front of the crown. "I'd better be going. Thought I'd stop by and say 'Hi,' since it's on the way home."

"I understand. I have to get back to work myself."

"Bye."

"Bye," Dominique said, and turned to the computer. After the door closed, her hands remained immobile and slightly unsteady. She had been so sure that she was over whatever it was that had affected her when Trent was around. She had been wrong.

One glimpse, one smile, and she was back where she started—sinking fast, and not a life preserver in sight.

Trent got into his truck and knew five days away had accomplished one thing—made his body hungrier. Flicking on the ignition, he drove home.

All he wanted was to sleep for the next twenty-four hours. After the run to Ohio he had headed to Rochester, New York, then to Laredo, Texas, then back to Dallas. Every mile of the way Dominique had ridden with him. At night she was there when he went to sleep, and she was waiting for him when he woke up. The past five days were the loneliest he had ever spent.

Now he was back, and wishing he hadn't gone. He didn't like the shadows in her eyes. He planned a little talk with Janice to see how Dominique's business was going.

Something told him it *wasn't*. If there was anything he could do to help, it was as good as done. Helping her out wouldn't hurt anything. They weren't dating or anything.

Once home, he showered and plopped down nude across his king-size bed. He had just settled his body comfortably when the phone rang.

He ignored the sound, knowing the answering machine would pick it up, and wished he had unplugged the thing. He was too tired to talk to anyone, and if it was business his staff could run things as well as he.

"Trent, this is Frank Lloyd. Just wanted to remind you that my wife and I are looking forward to seeing you and your guest Thursday night at the dinner party. Please call."

Trent groaned into the pillow as the answering machine clicked off. Lloyd was a business associate and a friend. He owned the company that had supplied Trent with diesel fuel at a very reasonable rate for the past five years. Since diesel was Trent's highest outlay, he liked to keep Frank Lloyd happy.

Showing up without a woman on his arm tomorrow night was definitely not going to win points. Scowling, he rolled onto his back. He hadn't dated in months. Had no desire to do so.

But he needed a woman.

One popped into his mind. Instead of his scowl deepening, he smiled, tired of fighting the inevitable. There was only one woman he wanted to take out, and somehow he was going to make it happen.

Dominique Everette broke just about every rule he had about women: She was struggling in her business. Worse, she interfered in his business. But something told him she was well worth the risks involved.

With a smile on his face, he rolled onto his side and went to sleep.

Chapter Six

"Good morning, Janice," Trent said Thursday morning as he strolled into her office at the antique store, trying to be casual. He was anything but.

"Good morning, Trent." She greeted him with a smile, resting her silk-clad arms on the papers strewn over the wide surface of the Chippendale desk, which was polished to a high sheen. "Dominique told me you were home."

"I need your help." He didn't believe in wasting time.

Since awakening that morning he thought of little else except how to get Dominique to go with him tonight. He was convinced that a straightforward approach, his usual way, wouldn't work this time. Breaking another rule seemed par for the course.

Janice frowned. "I knew something was bothering you. I called last night, but got your machine."

"I was beat from the trip. Sorry."

"That's all right. I simply wanted to invite you over for

dinner," Janice assured him. "As for my help, you know you only have to ask."

Trent lifted his cap, then ran his large hand across his head. Now came the hard part. "I hate to put you in this position, but I can't figure out another way," he admitted, then proceeded to pace on the Aubusson rug in front of her desk.

Janice's worry and concern deepened. Trent was always calm no matter the circumstances. "It can't be that bad."

Stopping, Trent looked at her with true desperation in his dark brown eyes. "I need your to help get me a date for tonight."

She relaxed. "Trent, you should be ashamed of yourself for scaring me. Any young woman you know would be happy to go out with you."

"Yeah, but they'd expect me to call again. I need a date with no strings." Placing both hands on the desk, he stared across the surface at her. "That's why I need you to help me."

Her shoulders pressed against the high back of the woven, upholstered chair. "Me?"

"I know you've sometimes matched up a few neighbors and friends. I thought you might help me out."

Janice lowered her gaze and began straightening the papers on her desk. "I don't know where you could have heard such a thing."

"Come on, Janice. I wouldn't ask if I didn't need your help," Trent admitted. "Mr. Scoggins stopped by the house last fall while he was out for a walk and decided to stay and watch a football game with me. He had one too many beers cheering the Cowboys on to a victory against the Redskins, and told me everything."

That got her attention. She lifted her head. "And just what is everything?"

Trent straightened. "That you have an unofficial dating service for people over fifty called No Strings. You've met a lot of your clients through your business. It's very exclusive and private."

"Apparently not private enough."

"Please don't be upset with Mr. Scoggins," Trent said. "As I said, he had one too many beers. I gathered he's very pleased with a Mrs. Taylor who lives in East Dallas. I just hope you can do the same for me. On a one-time basis, of course."

Janice settled back in her chair. "Trent, you said it yourself. I deal with people over fifty."

Trent shoved his hand into his front pocket. "As desperate as I am, I'll take anyone at the moment." He sent her a speculative look. "You have any plans for tonight?"

Her perfectly arched brows lifted regally. "A woman, no matter her age or the length of acquaintance, does not like to hear a man state he's desperate and then ask if she's available in practically the same breath."

Trent winced. Maybe he should have gone for the straightforward approach, after all. "Sorry. You know I didn't mean it like that. I forgot about the dinner party tonight until the host called me yesterday afternoon. The last time I showed up without a date at a dinner party, the hostess glared at me and the empty chair beside me all evening."

"Surely you can explain to him that your date had to cancel," Janice offered.

"I could, except it wouldn't be the truth. In any case some of the people coming tonight were at a dinner party last month, and I didn't have a date then either. I always intend to invite someone, then I get busy and forget."

"Freud said there are no accidents, Trent."

Broad shoulders shrugged. "Maybe. I told you I don't

have time to keep a woman happy. I'm too busy with my business. Anyway, Mr. Lloyd, tonight's host, made it a point when I returned his call today to mention that his wife hoped the same thing didn't happen tonight.''

"Then cancel entirely," Janice suggested.

"I tried. No go." Trent shook his dark head, glad he didn't have to fabricate this part. "Mr. Lloyd said his wife had gone to a lot of trouble and wanted everything to run smoothly. Two empty seats would be upsetting."

Entwining her fingers, Janice braced her arms on her desk. "How important is this man to your business?"

"Very," Trent answered. "Fuel is the major outlay in my business. Frank Lloyd in my only supplier, and sells me what I need at a price where I can still make a profit. If I lost the account and had to go to another supplier, I wouldn't get as good a deal."

She peered at him closely. "But is he the vindictive type?"

"I don't think so, but I don't think his call yesterday was a coincidence, either," he said slowly.

"A warning?" Janice guessed.

"That's my guess." Trent moved a delicate Sevres porcelain figurine aside and propped a hip on the corner of the desk. "My guess is he wants to make sure things go well."

Janice eyed the entwined porcelain lovers to make sure they hadn't survived two-and-a-half centuries only to meet disaster a continent away from the factory in England, then switched her attention back to Trent. "I don't blame him. I have to say I admire him for wanting to make his wife happy. Do you know how much behind the scene planning and effort it takes to make a dinner party seem effortless?"

"No, I don't, but if she's going to get this worked up

about it she shouldn't have one," he said with obvious impatience.

"Being a successful hostess can be just as important to a woman as being a successful businessman is to you. She is often a reflection of her husband, and it is important that she shine brilliantly," Janice said from experience.

"If you say so." Trent stood. "Can you help me?"

"Sorry, I don't know anyone."

"You know someone."

Her eyes widened. "You can't possibly mean Dominique?"

"She's under fifty."

"She has also made it clear that she doesn't want any entanglements."

"Neither do I. That's what makes this so perfect. I don't have time to court a woman, and I don't want one to get the wrong impression when I take her out. This way, with Dominique, it's perfect," he said, knowing he was skimming the thin line of truthfulness.

Janice shook her head. "I don't know, Trent. Dominique doesn't do blind dates."

"This isn't a blind date. She knows me."

Both brows arched. "May I remind you that you two didn't exactly hit it off?"

"I know, but lately we've gotten along better. I'd ask her myself, but I thought she might take it better coming from you."

"So, Dominique was your choice from the first?"

"Yes," he answered.

"Mind if I ask why you had to back your way into this?" Janice asked, watching him closely.

"I wanted you to see how desperate I am before you said no automatically. Dominique would get something out of it, too," he rushed on to say. "The dinner party would be a great chance for her to meet some of the movers and shakers in the city. I don't think her business is going too well."

Janice bit her lower lip. "It has been slow, despite the referrals I've made. I don't understand. Her photographs are beautiful."

"So is she, and that could be a problem. Some women aren't going to want the competition. She needs to find clients who are secure in themselves and their relationships, who don't have to worry about paying their bill," he said.

"I suppose you're right."

"I know I am. All the couples tonight are successful and have been married for years. We'll be the youngest people there, and the only singles." His tone increased in excitement. "This could be mutually beneficial to both of us. All I ask is that you ask her, give her the facts, and let her decide for herself."

"I guess I could do that."

"Thanks, Janice. I knew I could count on you once you had all the facts." With a smile, he was out the door. It was only when he reached his truck that his elation began to wane.

He didn't know much about Dominique, but one thing he knew instinctively was that she wouldn't liked being pushed into anything. She made her own decisions. Trent had to admit that he wasn't sure how he'd react if the tables were turned.

Turning, he went back inside the shop. What seemed like a good plan this morning suddenly had flaws. Lack of sleep must have dulled his mind. Just as he opened the shop's door, Janice came out of her office and greeted two elderly ladies.

She glanced toward him and he shook his head and

retraced his steps to his truck. He'd just have to take care of
things himself, but how? One thing he knew—he needed a
date for tonight, and Dominique was it.

Dominique was at a low point. She had yet to come up
with a marketing plan, and the order for the sitting she
had done that morning wouldn't pay a day's rent.

She had to find a way to break into the overcrowded
Dallas photography market. But how? Leaning back in her
chair, she stared at the computer's blank screen as if it
could tell her the answer.

The phone and the front door buzzer sounded at the
same time. She glanced up to see Trent at the door. He
was in a black tux. Even from thirty feet away she cold see
that the perfect cut of the suit accented his muscular build.

Automatically she buzzed him in. Seeing his silhouette
in the doorway for a moment gave her pause. The formal
attire somehow made him appear more intimidating, more
dangerous, more sensual. Perhaps letting him in wasn't
the wisest thing to do. Trent made her body react in a
totally unacceptable way.

"Hi. You want to get that?"

Flushing, she reached for the ringing phone. "Photographs by Dominique. Hi, Janice."

"May I speak with her?" Trent requested, holding out
his hand.

"Janice, Trent wishes to speak with you." Her gaze flickered to Trent perched on the the corner of her desk. "Yes,
he's right here." She held out the phone. "She wants to
speak with you, too."

Accepting the phone, Trent said, "Hi, Janice. I decided
to take care of things myself. Thanks. Good-bye." Replac-

ing the receiver, he glanced around. "Things have really shaped up."

"I'm sure you didn't come here to talk about the studio. You were here yesterday."

He turned back to her, his gaze intent and more disturbing than any man's had a right to be. "Why not?"

He had her there. "You're too busy to take the time."

"A man is never too busy to take the time for the things that interest him."

Dominique felt her insides shiver. She didn't need this complication in her life. Her only concern had to be her business. "If you don't mind, I'd like to get back to work."

"Doing what, might I ask?"

For some reason she didn't want him to know she was floundering. Worse, she had no idea of how to fix things. "Working on a marketing plan."

"I'm pretty good at that. Maybe I can help," he said.

"No, that—"

He was off the desk and standing behind her before she could stop him. Her hands clenched as she waited for his derisive remark once he saw the blank screen.

"Just starting, huh?" His hand rested on the back of her chair, the back of his fingers brushing her arm.

"Yes." Unobtrusively, she leaned forward. Trent followed the movements, bringing with him the disturbing scent of his cologne and his own unique scent. Both had her wanting to lick her lips again.

"You have to show the public something different. Something unique."

Dominique propped one arm on the desk beside the keyboard. "But what?"

"Whatever sets your work apart from all the other photographers," he answered simply. "In my business it was consistent, dependable, honest service. My customers had to learn to trust me, and know that I was going to deliver their merchandise intact and on time. You have to show them that each picture is as important and precious to you as it is to them. You've got to sell your uniqueness."

Without thought she tilted her head and turned around. His lips were in her direct line of vision and mere inches away. She drew in a shaky breath and inhaled something minty. Jerking her gaze back around, she asked, "How do you know I'm unique?"

"I saw the pictures you took of Janice," he answered. "They weren't stiff, formal poses. They were fun shots. They captured Janice's love of people and life."

She felt enormously pleased. That was exactly what she had tried to do. Slowly she faced him, this time making sure her gaze didn't drop below his eyes. "Thank you."

He straightened. "You're the one who took the shots."

"And very few since," she finally admitted ruefully.

"That's because your work hasn't circulated enough." Facing her, he folded his arms, leaned back against her desk, and stared down at her. "You need people to know what you can do."

"I'm going to do an ad in the newspapers. I've already tried radio."

"I have a better idea."

She frowned. "What?"

"Take your product to the people. People see your product, but they don't see you."

She folded her arms across her chest. "I'm selling photography."

"Don't get testy on me. People respond to things beautiful and alluring. You're both."

She didn't know how to take the compliment. She did know that for the first time in years she was thankful for the way she looked. "I want my work to speak for itself."

"It will, but you have to get them to look first. I have the perfect solution," he told her, coming around to the front of the desk and staring down at her.

Warily, he eyed the tux. "Does the way you're dressed have anything to do with it?"

"Always knew you were smart."

"And busy. So if you'll just tell me what this is all about, I can get back to work."

"And impatient," he rushed on when she frowned, "I have an important dinner party to attend tonight and I need a da—"

"I don't have time to date," she said, cutting him off.

"Neither do I. That's why I'm asking you."

Surprise was clearly written on her face.

His smile made her want to hit him. "The dinner party tonight is strictly business. I had asked Janice to speak to you for me, then I decided to ask myself."

She folded her arms. "Why?"

"I didn't want you to feel as if you were under an obligation to go, or think I was pushing you," he answered truthfully. "We're still testing the waters of our friendship, and I didn't want them muddied."

That hadn't been what she wanted to know. "Why didn't you get your own date?"

He grinned like a little boy who knows he can charm any female who has a heartbeat. "Promise not to get angry."

Dominique definitely had a heartbeat, and it was galloping at the moment. "I promise to try."

"Fair enough. I work long hours and seldom have time for anything that isn't connected to business. The dinner party tonight is a case in point. Most women want a lot of attention, or are demanding. You take them out once, and if you don't call again their feelings are hurt," he explained.

"You aren't interested in me, so there would be no chance for either of us to get the wrong idea or of having our feelings hurt. Plus, I might be able to help your business."

He flashed his heart-pounding smile. "Believe it or not, I really am a nice guy. Janice said you needed a second chance without explaining why." He grew serious. "I own Masters Trucking because Randle Hodge gave me a second chance. I promised him if I ever saw anyone else who needed a hand, I'd pass on the favor."

"Sounds very touching."

"It's the truth. I don't lie," he told her tightly .

Instantly contrite, she said, "I'm sorry if it sounded that way."

"Apology accepted. Will you go?"

She leaned back in her chair and stared at him. Temptingly sinful. Her hands itched to grab the Hasselblad on the desk. She clenched them instead, glancing at his tux. "You must have been pretty sure of yourself."

"This is part of plan A."

"Plan A?"

"I was going to pose for some shots for Randle as sort of a joke. He's a great guy, and the reason I got into the trucking business. I owe him more than I can ever repay," Trent explained, then grinned. "He can't stand anything but his overalls. I used to handle sales for that very reason. But this afternoon I got to thinking, and decided you needed someone who could really draw attention to your work."

Just then the buzzer rang. Dominique looked around

Trent to see a mountain of a black man in the doorway. She glanced up at Trent in confusion.

He grinned. "This is Cowboy country, and you're about to meet one. Buzz him in."

The huge man didn't look like a cowboy to her. She shuddered just to think of the poor horse that had to carry him all day. Besides, he was dressed in what looked like a white silk, bandless shirt and black linen slacks. Definitely not the attire of any cowboy she had ever seen.

"Dominique, don't keep the man waiting."

She buzzed him in. He wasn't alone. Two adorable little girls who appeared to be about five and three years old were with him. Their outfits matched from the headbands in their short Afros to their shorts sets, to the abstract cuffs of their white socks. Each child had her small hand curled trustingly around one of the man's fingers.

"Hey, Man," greeted the cowboy. "My wife had to go on an errand, and I had to babysit. Hope that's not a problem?"

Trent reached up the long distance and slapped the man on the back. "Just so you're here. Isn't that right, Dominique?"

Not sure of what was going on, but ingrained with good manners, Dominique came around her desk and extended her hand. "That's right. I'm Dominique."

His jaw unhinged slightly. Distractedly he lifted his hand. "Pleased to meet you." The little girls took off for an old leather trunk filled with ladies' antique clothes. "You got anything in there they can mess up?"

"No," she answered.

"Good. Ready to shoot."

Her gaze swept over him again. He looked rather stiff and intimidating. Maybe if he were in his regular clothes—"You want to take your picture dressed like that?"

"What the matter with the way I'm dressed?" he said, not sounding at all pleased.

"Nothing," she hastened to reassure the towering man.

"He looks fine, Dominique," Trent said, almost glaring at her.

"Of course he does," she said to Trent, then faced the man glaring down at her and swallowed. "Trent said you were a cowboy, and I just thought you'd want to have your picture taken in your boots, or at least your Stetson."

Both men stared at Dominique for what seemed countless moments, then met each other's gazes and burst out laughing. Dominique suddenly felt as if she were the brunt of a joke. "Did I say something funny?"

"Not at all," Trent said, struggling to stop laughing. "It's my fault for not making the introductions sooner." Trent quickly corrected the matter. Dominique's expression didn't change.

He and the man exchanged looks again. "You still have no idea who he is, do you?"

"I'm sorry if you're someone I should recognize," she said, knowing how some people's egos were easily bruised when the world didn't know them. "I've been out of touch lately."

"You'd have to have been out of the country not to know about the world champion Dallas Cowboys, and one of their star team members," Trent offered.

She had been in Europe, but didn't think this was the time to tell Trent.

"That's all ri—girls, get out of there."

Dominique turned to watch the man move with surprising speed and agility toward the two giggling girls who were in a tangle of clothes and beads. Scooping up one in each arm, he faced her.

The oldest child had a three-foot strand of pearls dangling around her neck; her hand was clamped on the wide brim of a ladies' straw hat encircled in large poppies. The youngest had a ladies' shoe dangling from her foot, a pink boa around her neck.

"Sorry, Dominique. I'll pay for any damage to the clothes and other things."

Dominique wasn't thinking about damages. The brawny man holding the two small, giggling girls so tenderly was such a contrast that she knew she had to capture the moment. Reaching for her Hasselblad 503CW, she raised the viewfinder to her eye. The adjustments were smooth, automatic. The motordrive whirled as she took several rapid shots.

The camera lowered. "Please, sit down with the girls in front of the trunk."

He did so easily, attesting to his strength and also to ease of practice. Here was a loving father who took time with his children. That was what she wanted to capture.

She knew she was right about the relationship as she watched the youngest cup her father's face with her small hands and kiss him while the oldest leaned contentedly against his wide chest. The camera shutter whirred and whirred.

Ten minutes and seventy-two shots later, she sat back on her booted heels, a satisfied smile on her face. "You have two precious daughters."

He beamed and hugged the giggling girls to him. "Thanks. They are something, but I thought you wanted to take a picture of me."

"Your children are an extension of you. Obviously you're a loving father, and that shows. That's what I want people to see."

"What about the Dallas Cowboys?" he asked.

"I know Texas is supposed to be bigger and better, and you've obviously shown it by being on the team of the world champions cowboy event, but is a Dallas cowboy really any different from thousands of other cowboys all over the country?" she asked seriously.

Trent's groan could be heard loud and clear.

Dominique heard the sound and forged ahead, anyway. "I simply think being a loving father speaks more highly of you than your occupation or anything else."

"So do I." On bended knees, he untangled the girls from the props and picked them up in his arms. "How soon can you have the proofs ready?"

She came to her feet, the camera clutched securely in her hands. The cost would double to have the slides printed in under seventy-two hours, but she had a feeling the results would be worth it.

"Anytime after noon tomorrow. You can come in at this same time if it's convenient," she said, feeling as if her feet were dancing a happy jig although they were still on the floor.

"Good. I'll bring my wife."

"I look forward to seeing you then."

The man looked toward Trent. "If these pictures come out as well as I think, I'll still be in your debt."

Trent stuck out his hand. "Why don't we call it even and start fresh?"

The handshake was sure and strong. "Thought you might say that. Dominique, I'll see you tomorrow."

As soon as the door closed Trent picked Dominique up and twirled her around. "You were really awesome. You know that!"

"Put me down," she told him, but she was smiling.

He sat her down, but kept his hands on her small waist. "You don't have any idea of what you've done, do you?"

His happy mood matched hers. "No, but I've taken some very good shots. One of them just has to be a twenty by twenty-four or at least a sixteen by twenty." She groaned as a thought hit. Her happiness took a nosedive. "Oh, no. I forgot to give him a price list. Janice's friend's eyes almost popped out this morning when I showed it to *her*. Do you think he and his wife will be the same way?"

Trent shook his head. "I can't believe you."

"What?"

"To you he was just a man and his children."

Her shoulders slumped. "I'm sorry I didn't recognize him, but he seemed to take it well."

Trent laughed, sending her stomach into another flurry. "The main thing is that everyone we meet tonight will know who he is. You're going to be the talk of the party. You'd better take lots of business cards."

Her eyes glowed. "You really think so?"

"I know so. Come on, I'll help you put things up so we can get to the party." Releasing her, he went to the trunk and began putting the clothes away. "I can't wait to tell Frank Lloyd why we're late. He has season tickets to see his favorite team play."

"Play what?" she asked, pressing the button to remove the film.

He didn't answer until he stood before her again, a mischievous smile on his face. "Football."

Predictably her stomach fluttered, but there was something else to be considered. One thing she had learned since her return from Paris was how seriously men in America took football—her father and Daniel included. "I'm ruined."

"Just the opposite," Trent said. "Dallas loves the Cowboys, and anybody *they* love. I'd say business is about to increase."

"Thanks to you."

"We're friends, remember?"

"Friends."

Chapter Six

Eyeing herself critically in the full-length mirror, Dominique admitted she wanted to look spectacular and didn't question the reason why. There was no guarantee that the afternoon's shoot would develop into a sale, but she felt like celebrating, anyway. The red silk gown she chose was sophisticated, elegant, and sensual.

Grabbing her tiny, red satin handbag shaped like a tulip, she strolled out of the bedroom. Trent was in the living room with Janice. He must have heard her because he glanced toward the door while bringing a glass of iced tea toward his mouth. His mouth gapped.

Dominique finally admitted the real reason she wanted to look good. If the stunned look on Trent's face was any indication, she had outdone herself.

"You look lovely," Janice said.

Lovely meant nice and peaceful, Trent thought. There was nothing nice or peaceful about the beguiling woman in red smiling at him. She knew her power, and wasn't afraid to use it. She was absolutely stunning. Evocative was another word that came to mind. A living fantasy come to life.

He had never seen a woman more alluring, more confident in herself. Her hair was loose and flowing around her shoulders like coiled silk. Hunger hit him hard and fast. He reluctantly admitted Dominique had a way of taking him farther, faster, than any woman had. It wasn't a comforting thought.

The glass clinked as he set it on the coffee table and stood. "I'll apologize early for staring."

She smiled. "It's the dress."

Immediately his gaze swept back over the gown that covered her from neck to knees but also displayed the flawless perfection of the wearer. His mind got him into trouble again—there wasn't a line anywhere to indicate undergarments. He swallowed. Hard.

"Shall we go? I don't want us to be too late."

"Have fun," Janice told them.

"Goodnight," Dominique called.

Trent mumbled something, he wasn't sure what. Dominique could definitely be a problem.

Her skin is like warm velvet, he thought as he led her to his parked car. She smelled exotic and forbidden. He caught himself wanting to lean closer to inhale her fragrance, to touch her in other places to see if she was that soft all over.

"I thought we were going in your truck," she said, sliding in on the passenger seat of the roomy, champagne-colored Lincoln Towncar.

The dress skimmed up above her knees. He'd like nothing better than to place his hands on her sleek legs and slide the gown up further.

He cleared his throat. "Might have been a tight fit." She glanced up at him sharply. "Getting in the truck, I mean."

Closing the door, he went around and got in, hoping he'd have pulled it together better by the time they reached the Lloyd's.

He did, with Dominique's help. She was in a playful mood, and thirty minutes later when he parked in front of the Tudor style mansion in far North Dallas, he was back in control.

At the handcarved front door they were greeted by a servant and immediately shown into the living room. All the guests turned to see the new arrivals, who were twenty minutes late.

From the relieved expression on Frank and Ann Lloyd's faces, Trent knew his and Dominique's tardiness had worried them. He extended his hand. "Sorry we're late. Mr. and Mrs. Lloyd, I'd like you to meet Dominique Everette."

Even at sixty-five, Mr. Lloyd was a typical male. His eyes rounded. He recovered nicely. "Glad you could both make it."

"Welcome to our home," Mrs. Lloyd said graciously. "Let me introduce you to the rest of our guests."

The other four couples' reaction was predictably dictated by gender on seeing Dominique for the first time— the men with open admiration, the women with distrust.

Trent found himself annoyed at all of them, until he remembered his own reaction and noticed that Dominique didn't appear to mind. She was gracious and charming. When they were shown into dinner, she was complimentary of the table and the room without being effusive.

During dinner the women gradually thawed. By the time the main entree was being served everyone was chatting amicably. It didn't escape Trent that the reason was probably because Dominique wasn't paying any more attention to the men than they were paying to her.

They were male enough to enjoy looking at a beautiful woman, but that didn't mean they loved and cared for their wives any less. Finally Trent was able to relax enough to enjoy his succulent prime rib and baby potatoes.

They were finishing dessert when Mr. Lloyd gave Trent the opening he had been waiting for all evening. "My box is open to any of you who want to come and watch the Cowboys beat up on the Philadelphia Eagles Monday night. Should be a massacre," he said gleefully.

Ann shot him a pained look. Her husband grinned. Ruefully shaking her head, she asked, "What did you men do before football?"

Frank shook his head of graying hair. "I don't even want to think about it."

Everyone laughed.

Trent placed his fork on the empty dessert plate where there had been a large wedge of pecan pie and took the plunge. "Dominique, for one, is glad. Her latest client plays for the Cowboys."

All eyes turned to her. "Trent, why don't *you* tell them?" she suggested easily.

He was only too happy to give them the details. "I had seen the fantastic pictures Dominique took of her godmother and I suggested he come by. But Dominique took one look at his daughters playing dress up and decided to do a family shot."

All eyes focused on her again. "They were about three and five years-old, and just precious," she said. "I can't wait until I see the prints."

"Neither could he. He's coming back with his wife tomorrow afternoon," Trent said.

"Are portraits your specialty?" one of the other dinner guests asked.

"Yes, but I don't like formal poses. I'd much rather create something unique that says something about the individual," Dominique explained. "The photos this afternoon just happened. It wasn't planned, but that's what is going to make them great."

"How do you know?" asked the man to her left, who was vice-president of a bank.

"I just know. The way a tennis player knows a particular shot is going to win the game. The way you know when the stock is going to plunge or rise. You just know," she said simply.

He nodded. "I have a six-year-old grandson who loves to fish more than eat. What do you think would fit him?"

"A tattered straw hat, old-fashioned overalls rolled up midway on his legs, a cane fishing pole in one hand, and a tin minnow bucket in the other."

"Oh," said the perfectly coiffured woman in a black gown beside him.

Dominique flushed. "Sorry. I didn't mean to offend you by mentioning the bait."

"You didn't," the woman hastened to say. "I could just see Michael as you pictured."

"My son likes fishing, too," said the man across from her. She remembered him as an investment broker.

"Now, Charles," said the banker. "Our Michael already has the overalls, and I don't want his picture looking like anyone else's."

"Since neither of you have made an appointment with Dominique, I don't see how you can have pictures alike, and I'm sure you wouldn't get an idea and let another photographer take the pictures," Trent said smoothly.

"Of course not," they chorused.

Dominique caught Trent's wink and hoped no one else had. The odds were in his favor. She was the center of attention again.

She spoke to the second man. "Perhaps your son likes fishing, but he may have other interests. Reading under a shady tree, drawing, or perhaps he considers it his duty to find every puddle of water on a rainy day and making sure he splashes all the way through them."

The heavyset man laughed. "Are you sure you haven't met Ben?"

She smiled, as did everyone. "Although it's just my brother and I, I grew up with a lot of friends and family around."

"So how do you work?" asked the first man.

"I like to meet with potential clients first, to get a feel for what they like. The consultation visit is free, of course. If I don't come up with an idea then, I give the person a call later, when I do."

"From what I've heard tonight, I don't think there is a chance of having to wait." He glanced at his wife who nodded. "How soon can you schedule Michael?"

She saw no reason for being coy. "I'm open."

"You have a card?"

Her expression saddened. "No."

"Here you go," Trent said, handing the man her heavily embossed card. "I picked up some while I was in Dominique's studio this afternoon. I have some friends who are football fanatics who are going to insist she take their picture, as well."

"May I have one?"

"Yes, me too."

"Certainly, Ladies. Take extra if you need them," Trent suggested with a smile.

"Maybe you should have her do your picture, Ann,"

Frank suggested to his wife. "You know the children and I both have asked you."

"You know why I haven't, Frank." Ann turned toward Dominique. "No offense, Miss Everette, but my pictures don't turn out too well."

"Please call me Dominique, and that's the photographer's fault, not yours. It's imperative that the photographer not only have a solid understanding of their equipment, but of lighting and composition, as well. For your clear complexion I'd use soft lighting and put you in a setting that you enjoyed so you'd be at ease. My bet is it would be your flower garden."

Her eyes widened. "How did you know?"

"From what I've seen of your lovely home the rooms are marked by soft colors, fresh flowers, and light," Dominique said. "The botanical prints are as proudly displayed as the other pieces of framed art on your walls."

Dominique leaned forward to stress her point. "The living room is an easy mix of antiques, plush, upholstered pieces with pink pillows, and fresh flowers in china pots. Despite the elegance, there is a hominess that invites everyone to sit and enjoy. Like this room, it has richness and charm."

Obviously pleased, Mrs. Lloyd smiled. "Thank you. You're very observant."

Dominique sat back in her chair. "A photographer has to be a decorator, as well. The picture has to appear effortless, yet capture the essence of the people in the shot." She glanced around the dining room. "Just as the refinement here appears effortless, although I'd be willing to bet you put a lot of time and effort into creating the effect."

"It has taken me years of collecting to finally have the house the way I want it," Mrs. Lloyd admitted.

"You've succeeded admirably." Dominique nodded toward the French doors. "Decorative lighting outside allows dining room guests to enjoy the flowering gardens and terrace at night. From the size of those brass urns filled with pink geraniums by the doors, I don't think they were brought in just for tonight."

"No, they weren't." The hostess turned to Trent. "May I please have one of those cards?"

He passed one to her with a smile. "Something tells me Dominique is going to be busy, so tell your friends early so they can beat the rush. I'm thinking about letting her do me."

"How would you pose Trent?" asked Mr. Lloyd.

All eyes turned to her. For the first time that night Dominique didn't like the attention on her. "Doing something he obviously loves." His dark eyebrows lifted in silent query. "Stepping from one of his trucks."

It was obvious from everyone's expressions that they were disappointed with her answer. That was fine with Dominique. It was better than shocking them with her first thought—Trent stepping dripping wet from the shower, and not a towel in sight.

He was displeased with her.

She knew it from the stiff way he held his body as he walked her to Janice's front door, knew it from the implacable line of his mouth where a curve had lingered until an hour ago. His disapproval bothered her more than she wanted to admit.

She had every reason to celebrate and she thought he did, too. When they left the party a short while ago, Mr. and Mrs. Lloyd couldn't have been more amicable.

WE HAVE 4 FREE BOOKS FOR YOU!

ARABESQUE

FREE BOOK CERTIFICATE

Yes! Please send me 4 Arabesque Contemporary Romances without cost or obligation, billing me just $1 to help cover postage and handling. I understand that each month, I will be able to preview 4 brand-new Arabesque Contemporary Romances FREE for 10 days. Then, if I decide to keep them, I will pay the money-saving preferred subscriber's price of just $16.00 for all 4...that's a savings of almost $4 off the publisher's price with no additional charge for shipping and handling. I may return any shipment within 10 days and owe nothing, and I may cancel this subscription at any time. My 4 FREE books will be mine to keep in any case.

Name _____

Address _____ Apt. _____

City _____ State _____ Zip _____

Telephone ( ) _____

Signature _____ AR0198
(If under 18, parent or guardian must sign.)

4 FREE
ARABESQUE
Contemporary
Romances
are reserved
for you!

(worth almost
$20.00)

see details
inside...

ZEBRA HOME SUBSCRIPTION SERVICE, INC.

120 BRIGHTON ROAD

P.O. BOX 5214

CLIFTON, NEW JERSEY 07015-5214

IIIııılııılIlıılıılılılıılıılıılıılllılıılIlıılıılı.ıl

AFFIX
STAMP
HERE

That's why she didn't understand. That's why she was walking slowly toward the front door. "You're very quiet."

"Long day."

She stopped in the arch of light through the half-glass of the door. "Why did it get longer an hour ago?"

For a moment she thought he wasn't going to answer. Then he blurted, "Why couldn't you think of something more exciting for me?"

She blinked. "I beg your pardon?"

"I mean, you only met Mrs. Lloyd tonight, haven't even seen the children, and you came up with great ideas. You made me seem boring," he told her, digging one hand into the front pocket of his trousers.

"Boring?" Not unless they had changed the meaning of the word in the dictionary. He was mind-blowing sexy, with a hard, powerful body and eyes that could melt stone.

"Did you see the way they looked at me?" he asked, his voice irate. Then he rushed on before she had a chance to answer. "They probably think the reason I haven't had a date before is because no woman would have me."

She started to laugh, then caught his hard expression in the faint light. "You're serious?"

"Darn right."

"I thought the idea was good."

"It would have been if you hadn't suggested it."

"You're losing me."

He jerked his hand out of his pocket and thrust it toward her, his gaze running from the wild mane of black hair to her red satin heels. "You stand there looking absolutely sinful, and you want to take my picture getting out of a truck, and I'm your date."

The woman in her was wildly pleased that he thought she looked sinful. On the other hand, she wasn't about to let him know it. "Would you rather I'd said naked on a bear skin rug?"

"It would have been better," he retorted.

Her chin lifted. "I don't have one in stock, but I'm sure I can rent one. Will Thursday at five be convenient?"

"What?"

"Thursday at five," she repeated, enjoying the shocked expression on his handsome face. "I hope you're not shy, because as you remember I have glass on the front and side. I'm sure you'll attract lots of attention in the buff. Of course, I'll try to finish quickly—the air-conditioning is a bear."

Hands on narrow hips, he glared at her. "You're serious, aren't you?"

"As a heart attack."

The stared at each other for a long time. Trent cracked first. "I guess I sounded kind of childish, huh?"

"A bit, but then friends can be a bit childish with each other."

He reached out and brushed an errant curl away from her face. "Friends, huh?"

She shivered. When she spoke her voice wasn't quite steady. "Y-Yes. I don't know how to thank you for tonight, and everything."

He chuckled, his good humor returning. "I thought they were going to come to blows over you."

Her laughter joined his. "I was surprised and pleased. They were really possessive and territorial."

He stepped closer, bringing with him the disturbing warmth of his body, the irresistible and forbidden allure that was uniquely his. "Being possessive and territorial where you're concerned would be exceptionally easy." The back of his knuckles skimmed across her cheek.

A painful memory flickered in her subconscious, but it

was no match for the sudden flare of heat in her belly. Her vision narrowed down to him, more specifically his well-sculptured lips. Air became difficult to draw in. His breathing appeared just as labored.

His head titled, bringing his mouth closer. Danger signals went off in her head.

Hastily she stepped back from beckoning temptation, but Lord, it was difficult. "I'd better go in."

Hot brown eyes regarded her intently. He wanted to touch her, caress her, kiss her. He wanted to feel the softness of her skin against his, to heat the surface with his kisses, to make her forget to be wary of him.

The last thought was the only reason he didn't close the distance between them and take her into his arms. He stepped back, giving them both space. "Goodnight. I'll see you in the morning."

"Oh," she said, her thoughts going back to that morning. She had jogged as usual, and had been keenly aware that he watched her as she departed and returned. She'd felt his gaze as if it were a tangible thing.

"Janice invited me over for breakfast."

"I see." She couldn't possibly be disappointed. "Goodnight."

"Goodnight," he said, trying not to howl his frustration.

Turning her back on temptation, she unlocked the front door and went in, glad somehow that Janice was in her bedroom. Entering her own bedroom, she tossed her purse on the bed and reached for the zipper in the back of her dress.

She should be elated about the latest developments in her business, but all she could think of was how sensuous and soft Trent's lips looked, and how she had wanted to feel them on hers.

A dangerous thought.

LaSalle should have cured her of letting emotions rule over common sense. LaSalle—elegant, handsome, suave, rich. At thirty-one, everything a naive young woman could want in a husband, unless he went into one of his rages— then he became a demon unleashed.

Merciless and cruel.

He had taken a malicious, sadistic pleasure in shredding her self-esteem, alienating her from her friends and family, and making her shamelessly dependent on him. She had been pitiful in seeking his approval.

All in the name of love.

He said he loved her, lavished her with expensive gifts, haute couture clothes, a luxurious home to prove it. The fault had to lie in her.

All her friends were envious when at twenty she had captured one of the most eligible bachelors in the country. She despised leaving her family to move to Atlanta, but she had hated the thought of being without LaSalle more.

Their June wedding had been a spectacular social event. She came home from their honeymoon on St. Thomas happy and wanting to please him in every way. She soon learned that meant dressing more alluringly and entertaining his business friends and associates on a moment's notice.

She was a trophy wife before she knew what the term meant—a thing to be put on display to ensure the envy of other men and thus the admiration of the man who possessed her. Her growing discontent soon affected her responsiveness in bed. One night, eight months after they were married, he went into a jealous rage because she didn't want to have sex. Positive she was having an affair, he threatened to kill her and her lover.

Then he forced himself on her, hurting her in mind and body. Afterward, he had apologized and begged her forgiveness.

The next day he sent her a double strand of perfectly matched pearls and flowers, and that night took her to an exclusive restaurant.

She forgave him, but she knew he had killed something in her for him that nothing could ever revive. He seemed to sense it, and became more demanding of her time, his jealous outbursts more frequent.

She tried, she really did, but she had not been brought up to equate cruelty with love. She knew that even with love marriages sometimes had problems. Her parents sure had their share. Yet not once could she remember them arguing in front of her and Daniel, or saying one derogatory word against the other.

A month later when LaSalle arrived home from work, she was packed and ready to leave. When begging had proved ineffectual, he had hit her. She had fought back, but it had done little good.

She had blacked out. When she had come to, she was tied to the bed. He'd free her if she promised not to leave him or tell her family what had happened.

She'd promised only to hate him until her dying breath.

Dominique came back to the present. Her hands were trembling.

She remembered that LaSalle had been courteous, a gentleman. Her friends and family had thought highly of him. Then he had turned and made her life a hellish nightmare.

Worse, the shame of her stupidity and weakness made it difficult to face her family, sending her on an endless journey of finding peace, finding herself. Finally, both were within her grasp.

Only another man was slipping insidiously into her life, though, making her feel things she had promised herself never to feel again. She couldn't let that happen.

She could handle friendship; she couldn't handle anything more. She never wanted to be that vulnerable again.

Sweat should not be erotic. But Trent's unruly body was living proof that it was.

That morning he had intentionally waited until Dominique went inside after her jog and had enough time to go to her room before he went over to Janice's kitchen door. His plan was to grab a quick cup of coffee and split. After a restless night, he wasn't ready to face the reason so soon.

After his brief knock and Janice's "Come in" he opened the kitchen door and felt as if he had run into a wall. He had calculated wrong.

Dominique was dressed in black leggings with a sweat-dampened, pink top that clung to her honey-bronzed skin and skimmed just above the impossibly sexy indentation of her navel. She must have had a good run, because more sweat ran from her high cheekbones to her soft chin before dropping onto the lush curve of her breasts, dampening the spandex material.

He had the irrational urge to walk over and lick every drop of moisture away. Very, very, slowly.

"Dominique, do you want a bagel or bran muffin?" Janice asked.

"Dominique jerked around, her eyes wide, her breathing uneven. "Nothing. I have a lot to do today."

Janice turned from the refrigerator. "Domini—"

"I'd better get going," she interrupted. "Good morning, Trent."

"Good morning." He watched her practically run from the room. He had probably embarrassed her by drooling again.

"Sit down. You're not going to grow any more," Janice told him. "Maybe you can tell me about last night. I fell asleep reading, and Dominique had gone for her jog by the time I got up this morning."

Trent had never known his hearing was so acute, but somehow he heard water rushing through pipes. Dominique was in the shower, naked and wet. His eyes shut.

"Are you all right?" Janice asked with a frown.

"No," Trent answered truthfully.

Pulling out a chair, Janice practically pushed him down into it. "Are you sick?"

"I wish I were," he answered, his gaze going toward the back bedroom.

Her gaze narrowed with understanding and unease. "Oh, Trent. No you didn't?"

"I'm not sure what it is I've done," he said.

"Then there is hope for both of you," Janice said, taking a seat beside him, her gaze direct. "Dominique isn't ready for a relationship. I'm not sure if she'll ever be. You push her and she'll run."

The question of "why" popped into his head, but he knew he wouldn't get the answer from Janice. He didn't mind, because he wanted Dominique to tell him herself. "I don't want her to leave."

"I believe you, and I know you'll do what's right for her. You're a good man." Janice stood, straightening her apron over her black skirt and zebra print blouse. "Now, tell me about last night while I fix your breakfast."

He did, glad of the diversion. This time when he remembered her idea for his photograph, he realized something he had missed last night.

Dominique might be attracted to him, but she wasn't ready to let herself become involved. She would accept friendship, but nothing else.

But no matter what they were telling each other, their body language was saying something entirely different. The heat, the need, the hunger, was there waiting. Simmering just beneath the surface.

Sooner or later it was going to come to a boil and they were going to become lovers. When the time came, he wanted no hesitation, no regrets.

Trent wanted her as wild and as hot and as needy as he was going to be. But just as much, he wanted her to be sure of herself, of him.

He wanted them to remain friends afterward. With everything in him he was determined not to jeopardize one for the other.

The best way to ensure that was to make sure she trusted him, trusted herself with him.

He sensed her return as if they were physically connected. He glanced up. She stood several feet away. She looked beautiful and a bit wary in a fuchsia pantsuit.

Her face said it all: he could have her as a friend or alienate her by trying to take it farther before she was ready. Somehow he knew she allowed very few people to see her inner emotions. The knowledge humbled him and gave him hope.

"I think you should eat before you leave. You're going to have a long day," he said.

Her grip on the wide strap of her purse eased. "Maybe you're right."

"Sure I am. That's what friends are for," he reminded her.

She took her seat and reached for the muffin Janice handed her. As the older woman passed, he felt her hand on his shoulder. She trusted him. Before he was through, Dominique would, too.

Chapter Eight

The phone was ringing when Dominique entered her studio. Hurriedly closing the door she sprinted across the room, tossed her bag on the desk, took a calming breath, and answered, "Photographs by Dominique, Dominique speaking. How may I help you?"

After a warm greeting, Samuel Jacobs, the banker she had met the night before, quickly got down to business. He wanted to schedule an appointment for his grandson and granddaughter. He and his wife didn't want to show favoritism.

Five-year-old Gia was in ballet, and could wear her recital costume. They needed to know if she had the overalls, cane fishing pole, and minnow bucket for six-year-old Michael?

"I'd prefer you get the overalls. The rest I can take care of," she said, wondering where she was going to come up with the items.

"No problem. Is Monday at eleven still open?" he asked.

"Yes," she answered, opening the crisp, new leather-bound appointment book.

"Good. Please put the children down. Their mother will probably come with us. If that isn't too many?"

"Oh, no. That's fine." Taking another deep breath, she asked the dreaded question. "Would you like me to fax you a copy of the price list, or go over it when you come in?"

"You can show it to us then, but I don't really see that as a factor here," he stated simply.

Dominique gave a silent yell. She liked Mr. Jacobs's style. "I look forward to seeing you all Monday at eleven."

"Thank you, Dominique. Good-bye."

"Thank *you*, Mr. Jacobs." Hanging up the phone, she grinned and brought both elbows down sharply with clenched fists. "Yes!"

The phone rang again. She was almost afraid to hope it might be another customer. This time she was much slower in picking up the phone. "Photographs by Dominique, Dominique speaking. How may I help you?"

Mrs. Lloyd wanted to schedule an appointment. While they were talking, the line beeped for another call coming in, but Dominique didn't click over. She wanted each client to feel that when she was talking to them they had her undivided attention.

Ten minutes later when the call was finished, Mrs. Lloyd had scheduled a ten o'clock Wednesday appointment at her home for her garden photograph. Dominique was thrilled. Two appointments weren't going to keep the wolf from the door, but she had a chance to show what she knew. That's all she had ever wanted, a chance.

Opening the drawer, she reached for the yellow pages to look up fishing equipment. Before she could find the listing she had another call, then another, both from the other women guests at the dinner party. Coincidentally, their daughters were Idlewild debutantes, and they wanted something unique for their formal photographs in their white gowns.

Ideas formed in Dominique's mind while she was talking to each woman. She had no doubt that once she saw the gowns on the young ladies she could give them a photograph they'd cherish for a lifetime. Tuesday morning and afternoon were booked.

Hanging up the phone, she was ecstatic. Picking up the other yellow pages she turned to T. Finding the number, she dialed. "May I speak with Mr. Masters?"

"Whom shall I say is calling?" asked a woman in a slow Southern drawl.

"Dominique Everette," she answered, wondering how many women worked at the trucking company.

"Hi, Dominique. Everything all right?" Trent asked as soon as he came on the line.

"Hi. Couldn't be better, thanks to you." Leaning back in the chair, she smiled and told him about the calls. "My appointment book finally has something in it."

He chuckled. "I told you going to the dinner party with me would be good for business."

"Yes, you did," she said, enjoying the sound of his laughter and his voice. "I don't know how to thank you."

"Friends help each other."

"I'm beginning to find that out," she said softly.

"Stick with me, Buttercup. You ain't seen nothing yet."

"That's the second time you've called me that. Why?"

"You sure you want to know?" he asked, his voice wary.

"Yes."

"A buttercup is a wild yellow flower that is as beautiful as it is delicate, and can adapt and flourish in the harshest conditions," he explained.

"Oh." She felt flattered and immensely pleased. "I guess I'd better go. I have to find a place that sells minnow buckets and cane fishing poles."

"Travis Bait House on Lake Ray Hubbard should have everything," he said. "How soon do you need them?"

"Monday morning."

"We can take a drive out there Sunday and pick up everything you need," he suggested.

"You don't have to do that. Just tell me how to get there and I can find it by myself," she said.

"I'm sure you could, but the problem would be fitting the pole into your car."

She bit her lower lip. She hadn't thought of that. "I'm sure the salesperson will have some idea."

"Yeah. Stick it in the car and hope it makes it to wherever you're going. In the meantime, you're watching the fishing pole instead of where you're going," he said curtly. "I'm taking you."

She laughed, surprising herself again at her easy acceptance of his taking charge. "You're as bossy as my brother."

"I'd like to meet him sometime. Is he in the business sector?" Trent asked.

"He works for an oil company," Dominique said, uneasy about telling half-truths to a man who valued honesty so much.

"You have another call coming in. See you tonight." He clicked off.

Dominique clicked over to another call. It was the investment broker from the Lloyd's party. Minutes later his son was scheduled for Friday afternoon. Hanging up the phone, she smiled. Trent had certainly gotten her business rolling. Just wait until she told him tonight.

Her smile faded as she realized what she was thinking.

What she had done. The first person she had wanted to share news of her business turning around with had been Trent. Not her family, not Janice.

She could tell herself that the reason was that he was mainly responsible for the increase in her business, but she knew it went deeper than that. Somehow he had managed to do what no other man had done in eight years, make her forget caution and act instinctively.

Perhaps he had been able to do so because she didn't have to worry if he liked her for herself or her family's wealth and connections. To him she was Dominique Everette, a struggling photographer who needed a second chance. And he was determined to help her get it.

A man who thought of and cared for others without expecting something in return was difficult to dismiss. Add to that Trent's handsomeness and his knee-weakening smile, and any woman was in trouble. Dominique wasn't any different. She had been around wealthier, more sophisticated men, but never one who called to her in so many ways.

But there were other, more dangerous, reasons. She wasn't going to fool herself. He was attracted to her just as she was attracted to him. Yet, unlike other men in the past, who'd wanted to use her for their own selfish lust, Trent seemed willing to wait. A man who placed a woman's needs before his own was a rarity in her life's experiences.

But for how long?

Putting away the phone book and her purse, she leaned back in her chair. The question she should be asking herself was how long she could hold out against him and the yearning of her own body.

The answer wasn't comforting, and neither was the thought of what she had to do.

* * *

Trent leaned back in his chair, a wide grin on his face. Dominique had sounded happy and proud. He was pretty proud of himself the way he had maneuvered his way into taking her to get her props. Maybe after they finished he could take her ri—

"That grin is even goofier than the one you had this morning, when you came in whistling."

Trent rocked forward in his chair and stared at his secretary, Anita Tabor, in the doorway. Of all the people to catch him off guard, Anita was the worse.

Besides being on his case about finding a woman and getting married, she was an incurable romantic. Her eyes still misted when she found one of the notes her husband invariably left in her purse.

Anita maintained she intended to keep the romance in her marriage by refusing to grow old. She wore light brown contact lenses and kept her gray hair dyed a startling shade of red that matched her inch-long nails.

Trent didn't remember ever seeing her in anything that wasn't fitted to her mature figure. Today she wore a white rayon blouse with ruffles in the front and a straight burgundy skirt.

She was the best secretary he had ever had. She got things right the first time and could work independently. He didn't think anyone could beat her on the word processor. She had a knack for remembering facts and dates, spoke three languages, and her computer skills were almost as good as his.

He had always been grateful he had let his chief mechanic Herb talk him into interviewing his wife when she had lost her job due to downsizing. Today, Trent wasn't so sure. Anita had a tenacity for badgering until she got the answer she wanted.

"Did you need something?"

Her brightly polished nails clicked against the faux pearls around her neck as she advanced farther into the room. "To see how far you had gotten on that bid. But that can wait." She placed surprisingly smooth hands on the cluttered desk. "So who is she?"

"A friend," he said, leaning over the inch-thick bid proposal for a lucrative contract with the Dallas-Ft. Worth International Airport that was only a third finished.

"Does this friend have a face and figure to match that siren's voice of hers?"

"Anita, don't you have work to do?" he asked, turning a page without seeing what was written. Instead he saw Dominique as she had been that morning—sensuously alluring, her skin damp with perspiration—he had wanted to press his lips to every tempting inch of her. His chair squeaked as he twisted in his seat.

"Since you didn't deny it, she must have. So I guess this means I won't have to worry about you as much, or try and set you up with some of the women who have been bugging me for an introduction."

His head came up. "What?"

"Thought that might get your attention." She shook her head of shoulder-length, twisted curls. "Don't worry. None of them seemed right for you. On the other hand, this Dominique Everette sounded mighty interesting."

Trent went back to studying the report. Anita also never forgot a name. "She's just a friend."

"From that grin on your face earlier I'd say you don't plan on staying 'just friends,' " Anita said, giving him a broad, knowing smile.

His head came back up, something hard glittered in his eyes. "Dominique is a lady. I don't—"

"Don't go caveman on me," she interrupted smoothly. "You know I'll respect any friend of yours. It's about time you thought about something other than these trucks."

Trent relaxed. "Herb wouldn't agree with you."

A sultry smile played across Anita's red lips. "You wanna bet?"

Trent couldn't keep the smile from his face. Anita was as saucy as they came. "Get to work."

"So I don't guess you'll be taking any more long hauls in the near future?" she asked.

"You could say that's a safe assumption."

A frown worked its away across Anita's faintly lined face. "Watch yourself, Trent. You've been out of circulation for a long time. You're more likely to fall harder and faster, and be a lot more gullible."

He gave his secretary a long, disbelieving stare. "You can't be serious."

"It happens all the time. People aren't as honest and up front as they used to be, and it's getting worse," she told him, then nodded her head for emphasis. "So take it slow and easy. You're the best there is."

"You just remember what I said," Anita said indignantly and walked to the door. "There are no rules these days. I don't want to see you hurt."

Watching Anita leave, Trent dismissed her misgivings. No one was going to get hurt. They were two consenting adults. When it was over it was over—even as the thought came to him, he realized it wouldn't be that easy or that cut-and-dried.

But for the life of him, he couldn't imagine turning away from Dominique, or trying to stop whatever forces were hurtling them toward a foregone conclusion.

*   *   *

Several hours later he learned Dominique had other ideas. Standing in Janice's kitchen with a bouquet of flowers in his clutched fist, the happiness he had carried with him all day went from disbelief to anger.

"Dominique's in her room with a headache and asked not to be disturbed." Janice's usually direct gaze wavered.

"I see," he said, his voice stiff.

"She said to tell you she'd pick up the fishing equipment herself tomorrow," Janice continued, obviously uncomfortable with the situation.

"You tried to warn me," he said, his mouth a narrow line.

"Trent, I'm sorry." Janice laid her hand on his tense forearm.

"Anita did, too. Shows how much I know." Thrusting the flowers and bottle of vintage champagne into her hands, he swung toward the back kitchen door.

Janice wheeled around and stalked to Dominique's bedroom. After a brief knock she entered. Dominique sat on the Victorian windowseat, her arms wrapped around her updrawn knees, staring out the window. "These are for you. Obviously, he thought you two had something to celebrate."

Slowly, Dominique turned, her gaze touching the bouquet of pink roses nestled in baby's breath, the hand-painted, pale pink and white blossoms on the bottle of Perrier-Jouet. The knot that had formed in her throat— when she told Janice earlier she didn't wish to see Trent again—thickened.

There was nothing Dominique wanted more than to bury her face in the heady floral fragrance, toast the success of the day with Trent, hear him laugh, laugh with him.

Too foolish. Too dangerous. Her eyes shut and she turned away.

Little by little he was scaling her defenses, making her feel things she had thought she'd never experience again. She might have been able to fight the sexual urges, but the urge to share with him her thoughts, her dreams, was what gave her the will to shut him out of her life. He was becoming too important.

The realization scared her. Need made a person vulnerable. She'd sworn to herself that she'd never be at the mercy of another man.

"One day you're going to have to stop running, Dominique," Janice told her and shut the door softly behind her.

"I thought I had," came the soft reply. "I thought I had."

Seventeen short minutes later Trent strode through his outer office, his face hard, his booted heels crackling like rifle shots against the vinyl flooring. Ninety minutes earlier he had left with a happy wave and a grin on his face. Wisely, no one commented. More than one person looked at Anita, but the angry expression on her face didn't invite questions.

Trent slammed his office door, jerked out his desk chair, and flung himself into the seat. His mind was in a tumult.

What the hell had happened between that morning and this afternoon? She couldn't have been stringing him along. The thought that she might have sent a shaft of red hot anger through him before he dismissed the idea.

Something else was going on with Dominique, and he was going to find out what it was. He wasn't a quitter. He'd learned long ago to fight for what he wanted. He wanted

Dominique. He was coming out of the chair when his office door burst open.

Anita stood poised in the opening. "Haskall jackknifed outside of Richland near Richland Creek."

Trent came the rest of the way in one controlled rush, his mind clicking. The day was clear and sunny, the roads good. If Haskall had been hitting the bottle after he swore he had cleaned up— "Status?"

"Unknown. Haskall was carrying high-end office furniture. The trucker behind him called," Anita informed Trent, following him out to the driveway.

"Have Simons follow me with a truck. Don't call Haskall's wife until you have some facts to give her." Jerking open the door of his truck, he climbed in and started the motor.

"The driver who called said there might be a fuel leak. Richland Creek feeds into Richland-Chambers Lake." Anita had saved the worst for last.

Trent said one explicit word before pulling out. Rubber burned. He had thought the day couldn't possibly get worse. He was wrong.

Dominique couldn't sleep. After an hour or more of tossing in bed she had given up around one A.M. and gone outside. She should be sound asleep after such a wonderful day.

She was booked for most of next week, and the football player and his wife had been thrilled with the pictures and ordered extra for both sets of grandparents. She found no joy in either. She had no illusions as to the reason why, she had gone outside.

Over the six-foot cedar fence and blooming pink crepe myrtles, she could see Trent's dark house. Her slim arms wrapped around her. Her concern for him had mounted with each passing hour.

She had hurt him, and now he had more problems to deal with. The accident had been on the Ten O'clock News. Briefly Trent had been interviewed, his face grim. The cause of the accident remained unclear, but the threat of hundreds of gallons of diesel fuel leaking into the nearby Richland Creek and then contaminating the lake it fed into had local officials worried.

The cleanup of Richland-Chambers lake, if necessary, would be very costly, and would be the sole responsibility of the trucking company. Already contacted in Dallas and watching the situation closely were representatives from the Environmental Protection Agency. Frantically, she had switched the channel, seeking more information, but learned little more.

She didn't need to feel Janice's condemning gaze to know she couldn't have picked a worse time to push Trent out of her life. Protecting herself didn't seem all that important at the moment.

"Trent, why aren't you home by now?"

"I am."

Dominique spun around. In the half shadows of the light cast by the lamp in the backyard he stood silhouetted. She took two running steps before she realized she had been about to run into his arms.

Uncertain and uneasy now that he was here, she pulled the long silk kimono up over her bare shoulders. Trent's dark gaze followed the motion, then lifted to her face. She felt his searing look from fifteen feet away.

"W-What are you doing here?" she asked, her voice unsteady.

"Coming to see you."

Surprise widened her eyes. "Me?"

He nodded toward the light in the last window at the back of the house. "I didn't want to wake Janice."

"There are three bedrooms besides Janice's. How did you know which one?" she asked.

For a moment, his face harshened, then it was gone. "The wallpaper came in the evening before your first arrival. The hanger couldn't come on such short notice. I volunteered to help. After meeting you the next day, I realized why Janice was so anxious about getting everything ready for the room."

"I see." His statement only made her feel worse. He was one of the most thoughtful men she had ever met.

"I wish I did. What did I do to upset you?" he asked, taking a step closer. "I'd apologize, but for the life of me I can't think of a reason, and believe me, I've tried."

Shame and guilt slumped her shoulders. "Nothing."

He took another step. "Then why didn't you want to see me?"

She could run, or face the truth. "You make me feel things I don't want to feel."

In the dim light she could feel him studying her closely. "He hurt you badly, didn't he?"

He was too perceptive. "I don't want to talk about it."

"If that's the way you want it," he said, taking another step closer. "Why are you out here?"

"I—I couldn't sleep until I knew everything was all right," she told him, wishing she had the courage to add, "that *you* were all right."

"It is now," he said, and slowly closed the distance between them. His hands lifted, settling gently on her shoulders. He stared down into her wide, uncertain eyes a long time before he slowly, gently, pulled her into his arms.

Her palms flattened against the hard wall of his wide

chest, felt the unsteady beat of his heart, knew hers was equally unsteady. He seemed to surround her with his masculinity.

Instead of fear, she felt an inexorable need to press closer. "W—We were worried about you."

He rubbed his cheek against her tousled hair, the palm of his hands pressed against her back. "Sorry."

She let the pads of her fingertips stroke him absently through his shirt. She tilted her head back to look at at him. "Was it serious?"

"Could have been worse," he said, his thumb stroking her shoulder.

"How much worse?" she asked, barely able to string a sentence together with him touching her.

He stared down at her beautiful face, saw the worry she didn't try to hide. He didn't remember a time he'd wanted to share his thoughts—he did now.

"The driver wasn't drunk, as the policeman first thought. He was in acidosis from undiagnosed diabetes. The fuel spill was contained and cleaned up before it reached the creek. And, thanks to all of my trucks being equipped with air ride, the load didn't sustain any damage."

"You've been at the scene all this time?" she asked, knowing she should step away but enjoying the heat, the solidness of his body, too much.

His hand swept away an errant curl from her face before answering, "Most of the time. Then I went to the hospital to see Haskall. They care-flighted him to Baylor here in Dallas. I wanted to check on him and assure his wife about insurance taking care of his bill, and tell her that the accident was not his fault."

"Did you think it wasn't?"

His face hardened for a fraction of a second. "Yes.

Haskall had a drinking problem, but he swore to me he had been sober for six months. I gave him the short run to Waco to test him.''

Dominique felt the chill again. "And if he hadn't told the truth, and been drinking?"

Trent's face hardened. 'I would have helped prosecute him to the fullest extent of the law. Drinking and driving don't mix.''

"I agree, but something tells me more is involved."

"My customers depend on me getting their merchandise there on time and safely, and I depend on my people to be honest and conscientious. Any time one of those factors is in question, the company suffers," he told her. "I won't allow that."

"That was Haskall's second chance?" she asked, fearing she already knew the answer.

"Actually, it was his first. His brother, Carl, is one of my best drivers. When I hired Haskall, I told him one slip and he was history. I can abide almost anything—except a liar."

Dominique finally had the strength to move away. What would Trent say when he found out the half-truths she had been telling him? "I'd better go in."

"You think I'm too severe?" he asked.

"No." The answer came softly. In any other circumstances, he'd have her admiration. How many other employees would have given the driver a chance? "Actually, I think you're a very nice man."

He scowled. "That's a terrible thing to say."

Because she now understood where he was coming from, she smiled. "Not when you consider I haven't met someone like you in a very long time."

Everything in Trent stilled except his galloping heart. There were so many questions he wanted to ask about her past, about the men in her life, but right now he just wanted to feel her softness, inhale the light fragrance she wore.

"I was thinking the same thing about you."

"Is that good or bad?" she asked, a slight quiver in her voice.

His hands settled possessively on the curve of her waist. "Definitely good."

She licked her dry lips, her body trembling. "Trent, I—"

"It's all right. We'll go as slow as you need to," he said, his head bending, his lips brushing softly against her cheek. Then he released her and stepped back. "Thanks for worrying about me and staying up. No one has ever done that before."

Her eyes widened in surprise and sorrow.

He must have seen the sorrow because he said, "No one has ever tucked me into bed, either. You want to come over and make that a first, too?"

The words were said half teasingly, but the image of Trent in bed and reaching for her flashed through her mind. Heat splintered through her. "I think you can manage on your own. Goodnight."

Turning, she fled back into the house, closing the sliding glass door behind her. *One day you're going to run all the way to me,* thought Trent.

He stood waiting for the light to go off in her room, to know Dominique was in bed. Instead, the light came on in the den. A frown worked its way across his forehead. He had taken a step toward the house to see if things were all right when Dominique came rushing out, carrying something in her hand.

Breathless, her hair tousled around her face, she stopped in front of him. "I was afraid you'd be gone. I thought you might be hungry."

Trent felt an odd twist of his heart. He accepted the tray covered with a linen napkin with shaky hands. "I am. Thanks."

Moistening her lips, she stepped back. "Goodnight, and thanks for the flowers and champagne."

"You're welcome. Goodnight, Dominique. Sleep well."

"You, too."

"I will now," he confessed.

"So will I," she whispered softly, then ran back into the house soundlessly.

Chapter Nine

Dominique knew she was dragging Saturday morning and acknowledged the reason: she wanted to see Trent before she went to work. She had slowly jogged by his house, but this time she hadn't seen the slight flicker of the curtain or felt his gaze. Somehow the run hadn't been the same.

Returning home, she had showered, dressed, and gone to the kitchen. As usual, Janice was there preparing breakfast. While helping her Dominique had told her that she and Trent had talked and everything was fine between them.

Janice had turned from slicing grapefruit and given Dominique a hug and a kiss on the cheek. The pride in her godmother's brown eyes touched her. They both had expected Trent to show up for breakfast. He hadn't.

Janice had left at nine for her antique store. Finally, at nine-thirty, Dominique couldn't wait any longer. She reasoned that he was probably still asleep after all he had been through. She'd see him that afternoon, surely, but somehow that seemed a long time away.

Outside, she got into her car, tossed her purse onto the passenger seat, and backed out. The Jaguar had barely straightened when she heard her name.

She hit the brakes sharply, sending her purse sliding into the floor. Her gaze locked on Trent sprinting across his yard toward her in a pair of faded denim jeans, the tail of his open blue shirt flapping. His long feet were bare. He looked sleep-rumpled and huggable.

"Hey, I almost missed you," he said, grinning down at her, one hand on the hood of the car.

Dominique felt her heart rate increase, and smiled up at him. "Good morning. I'm glad you didn't."

His face softened at her admission. "Once I check on Haskall and the cleanup site, I'm going to watch the football team I sponsor today. Care to come with me?"

"What time?" She didn't even have to think. She had decided last night, when she handed him the tray and he had looked so stunned and pleased, that she wasn't running anymore. Such a small thing, but it had apparently meant so much to him. A man who could appreciate such a simple gesture could be trusted with her newly awakening feelings

"Around three," he answered.

"I have a few errands to run, but I should be home by two-thirty."

"Good. I'll pick you up then. I have to get the drinks. What should I get for you?" he asked.

"Bottled water."

"Any particular kind?" he asked.

"Anything you choose will be fine," she said.

"A man likes an agreeable woman."

"With the right man that isn't difficult," she bantered easily.

His gaze centered on her lips, then he stepped back. "See you at two-thirty."

Dominique drove away with a silly smile on her face, and she wasn't going to worry about it. She was going to enjoy her time with Trent and take one day at a time. If that broke every rule in her book, so be it.

Trent, in jeans, black polo shirt, and baseball cap was waiting for Dominique on Janice's front porch when she drove into the driveway at 2:45. Slamming out of the car, she hurried toward him. "Sorry, I'm late. Traffic was a snarled mess."

Standing, he smiled easily at her. "As long as you're here."

Opening the door, she waved him to a seat in the living room. "I won't be but a minute."

He laughed. "Somehow I doubt that." He laughed harder when she frowned at him over her retreating shoulder. "These games never start on time, so don't worry."

"It's just that I hate people to wait for me," she said, rounding the hall corner.

"Some things are worth the wait."

She paused, threw a smile over her shoulder, then quickly entered her room. She had already decided what she would wear, so it was a matter of throwing off her oyster pleated slacks and blouse and pulling on a raspberry-colored camp shirt and khaki walking shorts. Next came switching her handbag, jewelry, and shoes. Her room was a mess, but in less than three minutes she was back in the living room.

"Ready."

Trent glanced up from the magazine he was flipping through. His gaze tracked her from the raspberry sun visor to the colorful scarf tied on the strap of her purse to the white tennis shoes, then back up again. She had knockout legs that made a man's hands itch.

"Isn't this all right?"

"More than all right. You're beautiful."

Dominique blushed—something she couldn't remember doing since she was a teenager. "Thank you. It's in the genes. My mother's family is very striking. When she married my father, a full-blooded Muscogee Indian, it made an interesting mix."

Trent studied her intently. As if unable to help himself, he stroked the knuckle of his hand down her cheek and let it remain there. "Fascinating and exquisite would be more like it."

The reverence in his tone as much as his touch made her shiver. He smelled good. She wanted to move closer and wrap herself in his scent, in him. All she had to do was lean forward and—

"If you do we'll never make it to the game," Trent growled, his eyes dark and intense.

She took all her courage in her hands. "Would that be so bad?"

"I promised." His hand fell.

Dominique watched the need mixed with regret in his dark chocolate eyes. Here was a man any woman or child or friend could count on. "Then let's go. On the way, I can tell you about the fantastic sale I made with Bruiser and his wife, and you can tell me why you didn't mention his nickname."

Throwing his arm around her shoulders, Trent started to lead her out of the room. "If I had told you I wanted you to photograph a Cowboy named Bruiser you would have tossed me out of your studio."

"Point taken."

"On the other hand, the teenagers on the football team you're going to meet think Bruiser and his teammates are the coolest guys anywhere." Trent opened the front door and locked the glass door after them. "And when they learn you took his picture, you're going to be besieged by every player there."

Dominique's eyes widened.

Trent kissed her quickly on the lips. "Don't worry, I'll protect you."

Twenty-five minutes later when they arrived at Kiest Park, Dominique's insides were still quivering like gelatin in an earthquake. Trent hadn't acted as if the kiss bothered him at all. If she hadn't noticed the slight trembling of his hand when he put the key in the ignition, she might have thought it hadn't.

As it was, she was already anticipating the next kiss. This time, he wasn't going to get away with a little peck. Since she had decided to stop running last night after they met in Janice's backyard, she was rather anxious to see what she had gotten herself into.

She smiled secretly. Shameless and eager.

Trent cut the motor and glanced over at her. "That kind of smile has been known to get a woman in trouble."

"Only the woman?"

Trent's eyes blazed. The easy smile slid off his face. He twisted in his seat toward her.

"Trent, I'm glad you're here!" cried a happy male voice.

Dominique could almost read Trent's mind. It wasn't

pretty. But when he turned to the man approaching the truck, his voice was warm and friendly.

'Hi, Charles. All the team here?'' he asked, climbing out of the truck.

"Every one," Charles said, his gaze following Dominique as she rounded the truck and came to stand beside Trent.

"Dominique Everette, Charles Powell, the coach of The Tigers, the next divisional champions."

"Hello, Dominique," he greeted, taking off a cap with a "T" on its front and nodding.

"Hello, Charles." She held up her Nikon. "Mind if I take some pictures?"

"No. Help yourself." The older man turned to Trent. "Heard about one of your trucks, and know you had your hands full. I appreciate you coming."

"I promised to bring the drinks. Besides, I wanted to see them play," he said simply.

"You won't be disappointed." Charles slapped Trent on the back.

"Come on. We'd better get these drinks over there before they come looking for us." Easily lifting the large cooler from the back of the truck, the men started toward a group of loud teenagers.

"You know anything about football?" Charles glanced over his shoulder.

"Very little," she admitted. She had graduated from an all girls private school and college. Although Daniel had excelled in sports, his boy's prep school had only offered tennis and golf. In college he had concentrated on getting his MBA in three years. He succeeded with a perfect grade point average.

"Don't worry, Charles," Trent said. "I intend to teach her all she needs to know."

She glanced up sharply. Trent had a smile on his face

that made her knees weak. He winked and continued toward the bench.

Dominique slowly followed and wished she knew more about football. Like how long the game lasted.

Ninety-three minutes and counting in the last minutes of the fourth quarter, she later learned. Cheering from the sidelines next to Trent, Dominique didn't mind. She was having a wonderful time. The thirteen and fourteen year-old boys had been predictable in their initial reaction to her; they had all given Trent the thumb's up sign.

He'd grinned and slung his arm around her shoulder. It was a good thing he had, because he chose that moment to tell the boys about her taking Bruiser's photograph. Suddenly she was surrounded, the entire team wanting to be near her, wanting her to take their picture.

Seeing their eager faces, she volunteered to be the team's official photographer and take all of their pictures. A wild whoop went up. The only reason she wasn't lifted up too was Trent's admonishment for them not to.

The Tigers had taken to the field and dominated it. Charles was right. He had a good team. Even with Dominique's limited knowledge of the game, she knew The Tigers played with skill and intelligence. She found herself cheering the teenagers along with Trent, and giving the referee just as hard a time.

When the clock ran out, The Tigers were ahead by nine points. Their side went wild. The coach was hoisted into the air. Trent picked Dominique up and spun her around. By the time he put her down, several team members were there, wanting to lift her up again.

Trent placed his arm protectively around her, a wide grin on his face. "Told you I'd protect you."

"My hero," she said.

"You'd better believe it," he bantered, then turned to a beaming Charles. "You think this calls for pizza?"

Charles's "Yes," was drowned by the team's roar of approval. "I can follow you with the team in the van."

He glanced down at Dominique. "You don't mind, do you?"

"No. They played hard."

"That's my girl," he said, giving her a brief squeeze before releasing her and picking up the cooler. "Charles, we'll meet you at the regular place."

Dominique couldn't resist. As soon as Trent turned, she raised the camera, lowered the lens, and clicked.

Stopping, he glanced over his shoulder. "What's the matter?"

"Nothing. Something caught my interest," she said, catching up with him. "I think it might be my best shot of the day."

As expected the pizza celebration was a wild, happy affair, with the teenage boys trying to talk with their mouths full and replaying the moments when they had shone and ignoring the times they fumbled or missed a tackle. Trent listened attentively to each player, his interest and concern for them obvious.

At the moment he was feeding the jukebox. Dominique had never heard some of the selections, but from the way Trent bobbed his head to the beat of the music, he had.

"He's good with the boys, isn't he?" Charles commented.

"Very," Dominique said, raising her camera to take a picture of Trent standing in the midst of the youths.

"It was a fortunate day for us when he came by the Y

years ago to become a sponsor." Charles nodded toward
the laughing group. "Most of them are from single parent
families and live in situations that would make most adults
shudder. Playing team sports they learn the value of hard
work and discipline."

Her camera lowered. "They also learn someone else
cares about them. You. And Trent."

The tall, lean man nodded. "But Trent is their hero.
He made it through the system. He has promised each of
them a scholarship if they keep their grades up and stay
clean. Only one kid had to be dropped from the program."

"What happened?"

His eyes saddened. "Joyriding in a stolen car. He said
he didn't know the car was stolen, but the rules for players
are clear. Any infraction with the law and you're off the
team and out of the program."

"Did you believe him?"

"Yes. I think his cousin Isaac orchestrated the entire
thing to get him thrown off the team, so his control over
him would be total. Isaac is a rebellious, angry teenager.
We couldn't help him at the Y." Charles slumped back in
the booth. "We might have been able to help his young
cousin, Jessie. He's a good kid. Trent liked the boy. It tore
him up to put Jessie off the team. But rules are rules. You
start bending them for one, and discipline is shot to hell."

"Where is he now?" she asked.

"Following Isaac straight to the pen or an early grave.
They live in the area, as do the other kids." Leaning forward, he twisted the paper his straw came in. "Isaac is an
accident waiting to happen. Unfortunately, when it does
Jessie is going to be right along beside him."

"Hey, why the long faces?" Trent asked, sliding in the
booth beside her.

"I was telling her about Isaac and Jessie," Charles explained.

The smile faded from Trent's face. "Isaac is going to drag Jessie right along with him until they're of age, and then some judge is going to throw the book at them both. If they live that long."

"Can't you do anything?" she asked.

Hard eyes stabbed her. "What? Until Jessie is more afraid of the consequences than he is of Isaac, there's nothing I can do. I've gone by there a couple of times, talked to his mother, but she isn't much help."

She touched his arm. "You tried."

"It wasn't good enough," he bit out.

"It was for them," she said, nodding toward the youths who were either clustered around the juke box, talking to a group of girls who had come in, or playing arcade games. "You made a difference for them. It hurts, but sometimes you can't save them all."

"I know, but I don't have to like it."

She gently placed her hand on his. "You wouldn't be the man you are if you did."

"Domini—"

"Hey, look at the babe."

Dominique glanced up to see four youths wearing oversized shirts, baggy pants, and sideways baseball caps. Gold chains glittered around their necks. The oldest appeared to be about seventeen or eighteen, with a scraggly goatee. Beside her, Trent tensed.

"You want a real man, Honey, to rock your world."

Trent came out of the booth in a rush. Grinning, the young man who had spoken held up his hands. "Be cool, Dude. Be cool."

"One day, if we're both lucky, you're going to reach adulthood and I'll be waiting," Trent said.

The teenager chuckled and glanced around the restaurant. "Did you hear this old man threaten me? I oughta call the cops."

"You mean you know your numbers, Isaac?" Trent asked mildly.

Laughter erupted in the restaurant, then ebbed just as quickly when Isaac turned toward the sound. His brown eyes narrowed, he faced Trent again. "Watch it, Old Man. I might forget my mama taught me to respect my elders." He snickered and glanced around. "I forgot you wouldn't know anything about *that*, since your mama threw you away like trash."

Dominique gasped and tried to come out of the booth. Trent blocked her way and it was like trying to move the bolted down booth.

Charles had no such problem. "Say another word, Isaac, and I'll gladly spend the night in jail," he warned.

Dominique glared over Trent's rigid shoulder. "Leave him alone!"

"You let everybody do your fighting for you, Old Man." Isaac sneered. "See, Jessie, he ain't nothing, just like I said."

An overweight black teenager with a cherubic face glanced at them, then away. Head bowed, he dug both hands into his pockets.

Isaac didn't notice. He was too busy looking Trent up and down in distaste. He sneered again. "Ain't nothing. I could screw the bitc—"

Trent struck without warning. Isaac found himself a foot off the floor, Trent's hand clutching the collar of his jersey. His eyes bugged, then watered. Only a strangled gasp managed to slip past his gasping lips.

"Trent. Trent, please," Dominique pleaded, trying to

peel Trent's hand away from Isaac's neck without success. No one else moved. "Trent, please."

"I hate to do this, but she's right, Mr. Masters."

Dominique turned to see two policemen coming toward them. Relief surged through her until she thought of the consequences. "He was provoked."

"Never doubted it, Miss," said the older of the two— Officer Bolder was on his gold nameplate. "Mr. Masters, he's going to pass out in a second and we're going to have to take him to the hospital, and there's going to be a lot of paperwork. I hate doing paperwork. Keeps me off my beat."

"Trent, *please!*" Dominique pleaded.

His hand opened. Isaac crumpled to the floor. Gasping for breath, he held both hands to his throat.

"I can either assume Mr. Masters was teaching you a new judo technique, or there was some type of altercation," said Officer Bolden. Isaac was already nodding his head.

"If there was an altercation your parole officer would have to be notified. I'd have to take statements from all the witnesses involved, and if I learned you caused this in any way, I'm positive your parole officer would consider it a clear violation of your parole, and back in juvenile you'd go."

The policeman looked thoughtful. "Then again, your overworked parole officer might decide he's tired of fooling with you and let you be classified as an adult, and off to Lew Sterrett jail you'd go. Seems I remember from all our associations that you turned seventeen last week, and to the courts you're now considered an adult."

Trent moved. The second policeman stepped in front of him.

"Your call, Isaac," Officer Bolden said.

The young man grabbed his baseball cap from the floor,

then pulled himself to his feet. His old eyes were savage and promised retribution. His gaze moved past Trent, who towered a good five inches over the policeman, to Dominique by his side.

"You made a mistake, Old Man." Holding his throat, he shoved his way through the crowd that parted to allow him to pass. Silently the three youths with him followed. The youngest and heaviest of the three stopped and stared back at Trent briefly, then followed the others.

"The action is over, folks. Take your seats," the policeman ordered, then said, "Charles, why don't you get the boys together and take them home?"

"I'll call you later, Trent." With a slight squeeze of the younger man's arm, Charles passed and motioned for the players. They were almost out the door before Trent moved.

The policemen and Dominique followed closely. Trent stopped in front of the group of wide-eyed teenagers.

"I broke a rule. What I did was wrong. I let my temper get the best of me. That's not how you settle differences. Violence creates problems, not solve them," he said. "If Sergeant Bolden weren't a good man, I'd be in trouble and off the team. I wouldn't have liked that."

"We understand, Mr. Masters," said Kent, the captain and quarterback of The Tigers. "You couldn't let Isaac call Miss Everette out of her name. A man's got to protect his woman. We'll see you at practice next week if you can make it." He held up his hand, palm out.

Trent slapped the palm, then in turn each of the subsequent players'.

"I told you you made a difference," Dominique said, taking his arm as the last player left the restaurant. He flinched. She frowned up at him. "Trent?"

His face grim, he turned to the policeman. "Sorry, Officer Bolden."

"Like the lady said, you were provoked. Why don't you take her home so the place can get back to normal?" he suggested.

"Did you just happen by, or did someone call you?" Trent asked, not moving.

"The manager. Now, good-bye."

Nodding, he closed his fingers loosely around Dominique's arm, then led her from the restaurant. Outside he opened the door of his truck and helped her in. Without a word he came around, started the engine, and drove off.

Silently, Dominique sat in the truck, hoping to give him time to work through his feelings. He was angry, but she thought there was hurt and embarrassment as well.

A short while later he pulled into Janice's driveway behind her Mercedes. Leaving the motor running, he walked Dominique to the front door. "Good-bye." Spinning on his heels, he went back to his truck and drove off.

Dominique didn't move until the truck disappeared. Sighing, she slowly went inside. Trent was doing his best to shut her out. She didn't like the reversal of roles.

"Dominique, is that you?"

"Yes." Janice always asked the same thing, Dominique thought. She took another step across the marble entryway and could go no further. There was no way she could leave Trent alone and in pain.

Placing her handbag on the couch, she fished until she found her keys, took off her sun visor and the silver barrette holding her hair in a ponytail, then swung toward the door. "I'm going over to Trent's. Don't wait dinner."

"I may be gone when you get back," Janice said, coming into the living room as she fastened the sleeve of a figure-flattering, gold gown.

Her hand on the knob, Dominique glanced around and whistled. "You look fantastic."

Janice blushed prettily. "Paul Osgood—he owns the restaurant across the street from my shop—invited me to the Meyerson Symphony Center to see Porgy and Bess." She bit her lower lip. "I'm kind of nervous. It's the first time I've been out on a date in over a year."

"Wish I could give you some pointers, but it's been longer for me," Dominique said, then grinned. "But if it's any consolation, you're going to knock his eyes out."

Janice laughed. "That's the idea."

"Have fun."

"Thanks, Dear."

Opening the door, Dominique headed for Trent's house. Obviously he didn't want to talk with her. Too bad. They were friends. He was in misery, and she'd be damned if she'd let him stay that way or allow him to shut her out.

Chapter Ten

It took nine rings of the doorbell to get Trent to answer. His face wasn't reassuring when he did. From his imposing height of six-feet, brown eyes that had been warm and teasing before Isaac's arrival were as icy as his clipped voice. "Yes?"

On hearing the harsh sound she wanted to weep. She swallowed. Trent didn't need tears. "I'd like to speak to you for a minute. You can time me if you want."

For an uncertain moment she thought he would deny her entrance and close the door in her face. When he simply stepped back, she didn't hesitate to step inside. Her gaze never left his stiff, unyielding face, nor his hers.

There was anger there, but there was also something deeper, shutting her and everything and everyone else out. She thought of him growing up without the support of a family, and had to fight harder to keep her tears from falling.

How much worse would her nightmarish marriage have been if she hadn't had her family, if all her life she hadn't known that they would always be there for her? Whether Isaac spoke the truth or not, his spiteful words had wounded Trent deeply.

"Trent." She said his name softly, her voice trying to convey that she was there for him.

"I don't want your pity, or anyone else's," he clipped out. "Your minute is almost up."

So he didn't want to listen. Then maybe . . . Even as the idea of what she was going to do came to her, she realized she was about to break another rule—that of never being the aggressor in a relationship. She smiled.

Her slim arms lifted. She felt the tenseness in Trent's shoulders as her hands slid around his neck. His deep brown eyes widened, but he didn't step back. She took that as a good sign and closed her hands around his neck, bringing his head downward while lifting herself on tiptoe to meet his descending lips.

They weren't cold as she expected, but warm and incredibly gentle. The kiss needed to be just as soft and gentle and giving. Trent needed comfort from someone who cared, someone who thought he mattered, and she intended him to have it.

His past didn't make the man. He did. He—the man he had become despite now knowing his origin, despite tremendous odds, despite obstacles that would have crushed a lesser man—was the only thing that mattered.

That was her intention until Trent's body shuddered and his lips parted. Her tongue slipped naturally inside his mouth, tasting him, savoring the different flavors and textures and the pleasure. The unexpected shock was staggering, the need to dive deeper and explore unbearably tempting.

Somehow she managed to resist and lean her head back. Stepping away was impossible. His strong, muscular arms were locked tightly around her, keeping her flush against his lean, hard body. She felt him from the tingling of her nipples to the throbbing of her midsection, to the quivering of her thighs.

Swallowing, she stared up into eyes dark with passion and felt a tiny thrill of pleasure that she had put it there. More importantly, the shadows were gone. "Is my minute up?" Her voice was husky, deep.

"I forgot to keep track." This time he was the aggressor, eagerly taking her lips, her thoughts, until she was all want and need caught in a riptide of passion. She gloried in every sensation rippling through her body.

"Dominique," he whispered, his lips nibbling hers, then tracing a path to the pulse hammering in her throat. "You smell and taste like my dreams."

His lips came back to hers, rough and demanding, and she matched him effortlessly, endlessly. Warm, callused hands slid beneath her blouse and closed over her aching breasts. She shuddered, pressing closer, somehow knowing he could make the sweet ache go away.

Suddenly she was lifted. She had a fleeting moment of seeing an arched foyer and high ceiling, then Trent's mouth was on hers again, and with it came the mindless need and passion.

She sank back into his arms and their passion. She was as greedy for him as he was for her.

Then his mouth was gone and he was clinging to her, his grip almost bruising. "I don't want our first time to be this way."

Dominique slowly came out of her desire-induced daze to find herself in Trent's lap in a big, oversized upholstered chair. Her head was pressed against his wide chest, her legs drawn up beside her.

His large hand released its tight hold on her and stroked her from her neck to her hips, then back again. That wasn't what she wanted stroked. She made an inarticulate murmur of protest.

"Please, Dominique. Don't move. If you do, I'm not going to be able to stop this time," Trent told her, his voice gritty.

Dominique stilled, thinking of the incongruency of the situation. She had been the one running from a relationship and now it was Trent. Somehow in her inexperience she must have read him wrong.

Shame swept through her. "I—if you'll let me up. I'll leave and won't bother you anymore."

"You're not going anyplace, and you bother me even when I can't see you."

"I do?" she asked, angling her head up and brushing her breast against his chest.

"Dominique," he groaned. "Honey, please don't do that."

She eased back down, her fingers playing with the button on his polo shirt. "Then why did you stop?"

"A lot of reasons. Believe me, I still don't know how I did it."

"Are you going to tell me?" she asked, a bit of pique in her voice when he didn't continue.

"You have as much fire and temper in you as you have passion and tenderness. You're a unique woman."

Dominique melted against him again.

"I've tried to resist you, and when it didn't work I bowed to the inevitable. And before you get angry, no, I didn't think you were easy." His hand tunneled through her luxurious, unbound hair. "The attraction we had for each other was too strong for us to resist for long. It might have been different if we didn't live next door to each other."

"Janice would have been heartbroken if I moved," she said.

"I know. I wouldn't have liked it much, either." He sighed. "Janice knows I'm attracted to you, but she was worried you'd run. And she was right."

Dominique felt she had to defend herself and sat up in his lap. "Not for long."

His smile was sad. "I know, but that was only yesterday. Can you really say with all honesty you came over here ready to accept us being lovers?"

Dominique started to twist, felt an unmistakable bulge beneath her and stilled. "No."

"I thought not. You were coming to comfort a friend who is becoming more than a friend. But once we step over that line there's no going back." His gaze was searing, his voice gentle. "I want you like I've never wanted a woman, but I don't want to risk losing you as a friend, or to have either of us dreading coming home for fear of seeing the other, or one of us moving."

Tenderly, his large hands cupped her face. "We have to go into this with our eyes open and be very sure what we feel isn't going to wear off in a couple of weeks."

Dominique folded her hands in her lap. "I'm not much on relationships since my marriage ended badly."

"You're divorced? You want to talk about it?"

She hadn't talked about LaSalle to anyone since the weekend Daniel rescued her. She had felt too ashamed. "I was such a fool. I let him control me and humiliate me, and did nothing. All in the name of love."

Trent's eyes blazed. "Sounds like the fault was his, not yours. Love makes a person blind to other people's flaws. I thought I loved a caring, beautiful woman named Margo, thought we were going to be married one day. Turned out she was selfish and manipulative. The only reason she wanted me around was to help her father head off bankruptcy.''

Anger flared in Dominique's eyes. ''Don't worry. People like that usually get what's coming to them.''

''I'm not. She's no longer of any consequence to me, although it took a long time for me to come to terms with the situation. Overhearing her and her father talking about using me was actually the best thing for me. It caused me to leave West Memphis.'' His thumb stroked Dominique's cheek. ''Being married must have made it more difficult and much harder for you to leave.''

His understanding enabled her to tell him the rest. ''I kept hoping he'd stop being jealous, stop demanding perfection. I had finally had enough. Only LaSalle didn't want to let me go. He kept me tied to the bed for two days before Daniel showed up.'' Somehow she couldn't tell him of the rape.

''Where is he now?'' Trent asked, his voice dangerously quiet, his face savage.

''He died in an automobile crash three years later.'' She didn't add *a broken, ruined man*. Daniel had seen to that.

Once again she was gathered tenderly against Trent's chest. ''We don't have the best track records for choosing the right people, do we?''

''No.''

''We certainly know what we don't want, so choosing what we want shouldn't be too difficult. I'm holding what I want.''

Pleasure and uncertainty went through her. ''So, the problem is me?''

''Yes.''

An audible sigh slipped past her lips. ''After all the

doubts and reflections and worry I've gone through to get this far, you tell me I still have a ways to go."

Warm lips pressed against her forehead. "You'll get there."

"How do you know?"

"Because I believe in you, and I refuse to let myself think otherwise." He leaned her away from him to study her anxious face. "You're going to come to me one day with no regrets, no hesitations, and I'll be waiting." His mouth claimed hers, the claiming tender and passionate.

Afterward, she nestled against his chest. "You kiss very well."

"As the saying goes, 'You ain't seen nothing yet.' "

She laughed, as he'd intended. "You know you're setting a lot of high expectations in my mind."

"Good. It will keep you thinking about me."

"You certainly don't lack confidence," she said, sitting up to look at him.

"I learned early to believe in myself," he told her simply.

The shadows weren't back in his eyes, but she heard them in his voice. "Do you want to talk about her?"

There was no need to clarify. "She left me clean and in a new diaper and blanket in a hospital bathroom, with a note that said, "Keep him safe. I can't. Tell him I loved him. I did, but he won't remember." They think she was in an abusive situation. I work with a lot of kids. It's no secret that I grew up in foster care. Isaac guessed right that my mother didn't want me."

Indignation flashed in her eyes. "I don't believe that, and neither do you. Isaac was trying to hurt you in the only area where he sees you as vulnerable, the only area he has something you don't—a mother he knows. Don't let him succeed." Tears crested in her eyes. "Do you know how hard it must have been for her to give you up and not know if the people who found you would be kind, or indifferent, or cruel?"

"Shush. I didn't mean to make you cry. I don't think about her very much anymore."

Dominique heard the words "very much" and she fought to keep tears from falling. "Did you ever try to find her when you were an adult?"

"Yeah, but no luck."

"My cousin, Luke, might be abl—"

"No," Trent stated flatly. "It's over." As if to punctuate his words, he stood and sat her on her feet. "How about going to a movie, then out to dinner?"

She lifted a brow. "Is that how you end a discussion when you don't want to talk? By changing the subject?"

"Seems it might not work with you."

He wasn't ready, and she wasn't about to push the issue. She knew how difficult the past could be to look back on. "It might if I can have buttered popcorn, a hot dog, and a large drink."

"You don't come cheap."

"Nope, and don't you dare forget it." Lifting on tiptoe, she kissed him on the lips and started for the door.

This time she noted the polished hardwood floors, the Turkish area rug in front of the white traditional sofa, the rich bronze, floor-to-ceiling, custom swag drapes over sheers, the pair of graceful wing chairs framing the windows. Across the hall in the formal dining room, a sparkling crystal chandelier hung over a floral centerpiece on the double pedestal dining table.

"I like your place."

"Thanks, and thank Janice." He chuckled. "Once we got to know each other, she politely suggested my house needed a few things and volunteered to help."

"That's our Janice. I'll be ready in fifteen minutes."

"Dominique?"

She turned.

"Thanks."

"That's what friends are for." The door closed softly behind her.

The movie was a popular sci-fi one that had been in the top ten for months. The monsters were grotesque, quick, and deadly. The first time one popped out unexpectedly, Dominique screamed and wrapped herself around Trent's neck. Since her scream wasn't the only one she heard in the crowded theater, she hadn't felt bad. By the third time, she decided she liked where she was and stayed there.

"You want to see another movie?" Trent asked, his lips brushing against the top of her head.

"I'm enjoying this one," she said.

He angled his head down to look at her in puzzlement. Another chorus of female screams and a few male gasps went up. Although Dominique wasn't watching the screen, she dutifully buried her face in the side of his neck.

Chuckling, he kissed her on the forehead. "You're right. This may be the most enjoyable movie I've seen in years."

"Definitely," she agreed, chancing a one-eyed glance at the screen. Not a monster in sight. Smiling, she snuggled against Trent. They never stayed gone for long.

Almost two hours later the hero and heroine finally dispatched the last pesky monster, save one for a sequel. Trent and Dominique filed out of the theatre along with the rest of the audience into the cool night air.

"I still owe you, since all you had before the movie was a hot dog and a cola. What would you like to eat?" he asked, opening the door to his Lincoln.

"Chinese."

"I'm lousy with chopsticks," he confessed.

"I'm an expert," she said, getting into the car. "Since you protected me, the least I can do is feed you."

"You're on."

Good at her word, Dominique handled the chopsticks as if she had been born with them in her hand. Trent didn't like the look of some of the food she put in his mouth, but since Dominique was feeding him he ate it, anyway.

Too soon they were back at Janice's house. Silence fell between them as Trent cut the motor and switched off the headlights. Dominique pulled her lower lip between her teeth, her hands curled around the small, red, calfskin bag in her lap. Her legs shifted and the sound of her red gabardine pants rubbing against the seat seemed unnaturally loud.

"Don't get nervous on me," Trent said, his strong fingers circling the back of her neck beneath the collar of her white, appliquéd linen blouse and turning her toward him.

"I just don't know what to expect. What to do," she admitted.

"What would you like to do?" Her gaze went to his lips. "Come here."

She went. No sooner had his lips settled on hers than a bright beam of light engulfed the car. They both jerked apart. The lights shut off. Doors slammed.

"Stay here," Trent ordered and got out of the car. He might as well have been talking to the wind.

She almost beat him out of the car. She watched his tense body relax as Janice and a distinguished looking black man got out of a 850 BMW.

"Trent, who did you think it was?" she asked.

"Doesn't hurt to be cautious," he told her and curved

his arm easily around her slim shoulder and pulled her to his side.

"Dominique, Trent. We're sorry," said Janice, hurrying to them, looking beautiful and flustered.

"Please accept my apology," said the gray-haired man with her.

"I'm the one who should apologize to you and to Dominique, for acting like a teenager." Trent held out his hand. "Trent Masters, and this is Dominique Everette."

"Paul Osgood." He smiled warmly at Dominique and shook hands with Trent. "It's a pleasure."

"Paul was coming inside for some coffee. You two want to join us?" Janice asked.

"No thanks," Trent said. "I'd better be going."

"I'll move my car." Keys jingled in Paul's hand.

"Don't bother. I live next door. I'll just walk over in the morning and pick it up, if it's all right, Janice?" Trent asked.

"You know it is." Janice's gaze switched between him and Dominique. "Are you sure you don't want to come in for a little while?"

"Yes, thanks." With a brief kiss on Dominique's cheek, he walked away.

Dominique stared after him, and was glad she had when she saw him point to the backyard. With a secret smile on her face she headed inside. Paul, his hand on Janice's elbow, followed.

As soon as they were in the foyer, Dominique yawned. "Goodness. I'd better not drink any coffee. Nice meeting you, Paul. Goodnight to both of you."

"Run along, Dominique," Janice said, her look knowing. "I wouldn't want you to miss any sleep, or anything else important."

Trying not to laugh, Dominique quickly went to her

room, threw her purse on the bed, then raced to the
window and lifted it. Trent was there. Trying not to giggle,
she leaned over and he lifted her out.

"Do you think we fooled them?' he asked.

"No."

"Then we might as well make this worth it." His lips
took hers and the world around her receded. He was the
focus of her universe.

His tongue expertly probed and searched the sweet,
dark interior of her mouth. His hands were no less busy,
seeking and giving pleasure as they skimmed and teased
and pleased.

When both were near their limit, he tore his mouth
from hers, their breathing ragged and harsh in the cool
night air. They clung to each other until their breathing
slowed, the throbbing of their bodies dulled.

"Maybe we should have said good-bye for real." His lips
nibbled her neck, her ear, as if he could not force himself
to stop tasting her, stop touching her, stop kissing her.
"Neither one of us is going to sleep worth a damn."

"I—I could come over after she's asleep."

Finally he lifted his head. "No. This is the limit of our
sneaking. We're definitely not sneaking into each other's
beds. Besides, if I correctly read the gleam in Paul's eyes,
Janice might be spending her nights someplace else soon,
too."

"You think?" Dominique asked excitedly. Janice
deserved a man to love and cherish her. Funny, the words
didn't seem so impossible anymore.

"I think." Trent kissed her on the lips, picked her up
and sat her back inside her room. "Tomorrow after church
we can go pick up your props."

"Thanks for a wonderful evening, Trent."

"Goodnight, Honey. Sleep tight." He shut the window

and waited until she closed the latch and pulled the curtains.

Trent thought he might get used to seeing men get that stunned look when they saw Dominique, and hoped it would be soon. He wasn't used to being possessive or jealous. He was both with Dominique, pitifully so. This morning at church had tested his endurance, when men he barely knew had clustered around him after the service to greet Dominique.

Considering how fantastic she had looked, in a rose pink suit with a fitted short skirt, he had tried to remember where he was and not to glare at the men waiting to be introduced. It had helped that Janice was there, and that Dominique had treated them all with polite courtesy and nothing more.

But he had stayed by her side.

He hadn't thought that would be necessary at the small bait store on Lake Ray Hubbard he had taken her to after they had lunch at Paul's seafood restaurant with him and Janice. Now, Trent wasn't so sure.

Casually, he leaned against the scarred, plywood counter of Travis Bait Store, a twenty by fifteen wooden structure with a tin roof, and listened as the elderly owner told Dominique more than she'd ever need to know about picking out a cane fishing pole. She didn't appear to mind.

Considering Travis had a belly from years of drinking too much beer and doing too little exercise, a total of five, scrawny, white hairs sticking up on the top of his otherwise bald head, and only came up to Dominique's shoulder, Trent wasn't worried.

The other two men in the store were a different matter.

Both were in their early thirties, had all their hair, and

concave stomachs annoyingly displayed in their shorts and unzipped windbreakers, and—from what Trent could determine—were almost as tall as he was.

They had told Travis they had come in for lures. The only lures they were interested in were ones with which to catch Dominique's attention.

Not in this lifetime, thought Trent.

But they were trying. If he heard one more inference about how much money one or the other had made, or how fast their world-class boats could go, or about the customized work added to their new luxury sports cars, Trent was going to stuff cotton in his ears. Since there was no cotton in sight, he decided leaving might be a better idea.

"Travis, I really appreciate you taking time to help, but she just needs one for a picture. She's not writing a book on the subject," Trent said.

Both Dominique and Travis turned to Trent with a frown. "Information is never wasted," Dominique said, then smiled brilliantly at Travis. "You were saying?"

The elderly man's Adam's apple bobbed. He'd once told Trent while they were trading fishing yarns and sipping beer that looking at a beautiful woman made a man feel ten years younger. Gauging from the rapt way Travis was staring at Dominique, he had regressed to puberty.

"Excuse me. I didn't mean to eavesdrop, but did I hear that you do portraits?" asked the taller and more boisterous of the two men.

Trent came away from the counter. He couldn't believe the audacity of the man, but he planned to set him straight about trying to pick up Dominique.

"Yes," Dominique said.

Trent stopped midway across the room and glared at Dominique and the man. Didn't she know when a man was trying to hand her a line? He thought of lures, and his jaw tightened.

"What kind?" the stranger asked.

"Photography."

"She's buying a cane pole and a minnow bucket for a portrait tomorrow," Travis supplied, his voice rich with pride.

"Really," the man said, walking closer. "This is fortunate. My mother has been after me to send her a portrait. She's in Europe on an extended vacation. Do you have a card?"

Dominique opened her oversized bag and rummaged inside. "Sorry, I appear to be out. I can write out the number." Walking over to the counter near Trent, she took out a pen, scribbled on a small notepad, then ripped out the sheet. "Here."

"Thanks. You'll be hearing from me." He strode to the door and turned. "I almost forgot. What's your name?"

"It's on the paper. It's French."

The man glanced back at the paper, frowned, then smiled. "Oh, yes. I didn't see it." The door closed behind them.

"I'll wait in the truck," Trent said, his expression sour.

"I shouldn't be much longer," she told him.

"Take your time."

"Trent," she called as he reached the door. "Is something wrong?"

His gaze flickered to Travis. "We'll talk about it later."

Travis hadn't lived to the ripe old age of seventy-five without knowing when to make himself scarce. "I'll go restock the cooler."

Neither seemed to notice the store owner leaving. "That man was trying to pick you up and you gave him your number. He could be a maniac, for all you know."

Dominique folded her arms across her chest, tightening the yellow T-shirt across her breasts. "And you think I'm too naive or too stupid to figure that out for myself? Or maybe both?"

Trent had always thought of himself as a smart man— at least, until Dominique. How had he been put on the defensive with such a no win question? "I didn't say that."

"You implied it," she said, her black eyes narrowed.

"You're in that studio by yourself. I simply meant you should be less trusting." He tugged on his baseball cap. "I was worried about you. He had shifty eyes."

Dominique's lips twitched. "Shifty eyes?"

"He did, and when you schedule him make sure someone is there with you," he said.

She placed both hands on his chest. "I gave him a wrong number, and the words in French were 'no sale.' "

Trent brightened, his hands settling on her narrow waist. "That's my girl." The doorbell chimed and a customer came in. "Pick out your pole so we can go. I have a surprise for you."

"What?"

"If I told you it wouldn't be a surprise." Laughing at her mutinous look, he pushed her toward the cane poles.

Chapter Eleven

Dominique couldn't quite believe it when Trent drove beneath a sign that read Lowell Riding Stable. She stared at him, then back to the stables directly in front of them. "Does this mean what I think it does?" she asked.

"Why do you think I insisted you wear jeans and boots?" he asked.

She bit her lip, but laughter bubbled forth, anyway. "I thought the bait shop might be in a swampy area and you were worried about snakes."

"The two-legged variety sure put in an appearance at the bait shop," Trent said, and pulled to a stop.

"Hello, folks," greeted a bowlegged young man of about twenty, a wide grin on his face and an even wider straw hat shading his freckled face. "What can I do for you?"

"Hello. I'm Trent Masters. I reserved a few horses for this afternoon."

"A few?" Dominique repeated incredulously.

Trent shrugged. "I didn't know what kind of horse you were used to riding, so I reserved the entire stable."

She gasped. "You didn't."

He looked embarrassed. "Afraid so."

She threw her arms around his neck and kissed him before she could think of a reason not to. "Thank you. I don't think anyone has ever given me anything nicer."

"I was just thinking the same thing," he said, his arms going around her waist.

"If you'll come this way, I'll show you the horses," said the young man.

Trent reluctantly released Dominique and pulled her from the cab. "I hope he's not as longwinded as Travis."

Dominique curved her arm unconsciously around Trent's waist. "No need. This time I'm the expert."

Minutes later Trent knew Dominique had spoken the truth. She and the young man—who identified himself as the owner's son, Johnny—threw out words like *deep chest, strong foreleg,* and *long neck,* which all obviously meant something to them, but nothing to him.

The closest he had gotten to a horse when he was a child was seeing one in the pasture as he passed on the highway. His adult association was about the same.

"I'll take this one," Dominique said, stroking the white face of a huge, black gelding.

"You have a good eye, Ms. Everette. He's the best of the bunch," commented Johnny, opening the stall and leading the horse out. Head high, his velvet nostrils drinking in air, the animal pranced behind Johnny.

A frown of uncertainty on his face, Trent stepped back as they passed. "You're sure? He's kind of big."

"Don't worry. I was riding before I was walking. Did you decide which one you want?" she asked, glancing around the stables again.

"I, er think I'll just watch," he said evasively.

Her attention came back to him. "You aren't going with me?" Disappointment coated her words.

Somehow he managed to hold her stare. "No. I'll just wait here."

Her midnight black eyes studied him for a long time, noting his hands stuffed in his front pockets. She remembered his quietness once they entered the stables. "You don't ride, do you?"

"I've never been on a horse in my life," he admitted.

His calm words shocked her. "Then why bring me here?"

"Because you said you liked riding, and I wanted to give you something you enjoyed," he explained easily.

Warmth at his words curved her lips upward. She could think of few instances where a man had offered her pleasure that wasn't to be shared or didn't ultimately benefit him in some way—fewer men still who openly admitted that a woman possessed a skill they lacked.

Standing on tiptoe, she brushed her lips across his cheek. "Thank you."

"You're welcome." Lacing her hand with his, he led her to the saddled gelding. "I can't say I missed the experience until now."

Dominique swung gracefully into the saddle. Gathering the reins handed to her by Johnny, she stared down at Trent.

"What are you waiting for?"

"I wish you could go."

His hand rested on her thigh. "So do I." He stepped back. "I'll be here."

Nodding, she spoke to Johnny standing several feet away. "Can Rio take the fence?"

"Like a cat," came the proud answer.

"Now, Dom—" Trent began, but Dominique had wheeled the animal and was racing toward a white, wooden fence twenty yards away. He wanted to call her back, but prayed instead. Her unbound black hair streamed behind her back as she leaned low over the animal's neck and aimed straight for the five-foot fence.

He knew a moment of fear and helplessness as the horse started over the obstacle. For a nerve-shattering moment animal and rider seemed suspended in mid-air. Then they were over, and racing hell-bent for the next fence.

Fear turned to amazement and pride as Dominique and the gelding took the next fence as easily as they had taken the first. He heard her shout in triumph and watched them disappear over a hill.

"Damn, that lady can ride."

"You can say that again."

Fifteen minutes later Trent wasn't so sure about Dominique's riding ability. He hadn't moved very far from the spot where he had watched her disappear. Seventeen minutes after she had ridden away, he went inside the stable in search of Johnny. He found him cleaning out the hoof of a cinnamon-colored horse.

"Shouldn't she be back by now?"

"Hard to say. The ranch has thirty acres." Johnny never glanced up from his task.

Trent went back outside, only to come back three minutes later. "Saddle me a horse."

Johnny's shaggy eyebrows bunched. Releasing the horse's hoof, he came out of the stall. "Didn't I hear you say you don't ride?"

"I don't see where it would be all that difficult once you got on," Trent said, hoping he was right.

"You're sure?" To his credit, the young man didn't laugh. "We aren't liable for injuries."

"I take full responsibility for my actions."

Johnny turned and walked toward the back of the stable. "I'll get Bitsy."

Trent hoped Bitsy was as small and biddable as her name sounded. When Johnny led the small roan mare outside the stable, Trent breathed a little easier.

"If you're worried about Ms. Everette, I'll go look for her," Johnny offered. "But like I said, she rides well."

"I know, but even the best riders can fall," he said, the thought making his stomach knot.

"Not this time." Johnny nodded toward the hill. "Here she comes."

She came slower this time, almost at a lope, her hair bouncing around her erect shoulders. The sun was behind her, silhouetting her. She and the blaze-faced horse were a magnificent pair. Even as a nonrider, Trent could tell she rode well. The closer she came, the more he had the insane notion he'd like to be on the horse with her.

She rode straight to him. This time Trent took the bridle instead of stepping away. "You were gone a long time."

"I've been known to stay out for a couple of hours or more."

"What brought you back sooner?"

Throwing her long legs over the saddle, she slid down. "I kept thinking about a man who gives without asking for anything in return. I decided it didn't make much sense to think about him when I could be with him."

His hand gently touched her cheek. "I missed you, too."

She glanced at the saddled horse Johnny was leading back into the stables. "You were sending Johnny after me?"

"I was coming myself," he confessed. "I needed to know you were safe."

Her hands palmed his cheeks. "Except for the men in my family or close to us, I've met few men like you."

One hand closed over hers, his thumb caressing the back of her hand. "Is that good or bad?"

"Both," she admitted softly.

"I don't think so."

"Why do you say that?" she asked, genuinely puzzled.

He smiled slowly and tenderly. "Because this time you ran *to* me instead of away."

Realization widened her eyes. Reflexively she tried to draw back, but found herself firmly anchored against him, one of his arms securely around her waist. He had moved extremely fast and knew her too well.

"Don't get scared on me."

"The thought crossed my mind," she answered honestly.

"I know." Trent studied her face intently. "Just give us a chance."

She thought of her friends' failed marriages, her parent's rocky relationship until recently, and then she thought of Daniel and her promise to Higgins. Mostly she thought of the man holding her with equal amounts of strength and tenderness, and relaxed in his embrace. "I believe that's what I'm doing."

"You won't ever be sorry." One arm around her waist, he led the horse inside and handed the reins to Johnny. After thanking the young man and bidding him good-bye, they walked slowly to the truck.

Trent knew his jaw was slack, but he couldn't help it. He was human and Dominique was the quintessential woman, sensuous, alluring and provocative, and she was walking toward him in a bikini designed to bring a man to his knees.

The little white nothing had three scraps of material covering strategic areas and none of them wider than his hand. Worse, the bottom was high on the sides and scooped in front to show that incredible, sexy navel of hers.

He was trying not to remember thinking the first time he saw her how much he liked chocolate swirl, how much he liked licking it from top to bottom, but goodness, he was only a man. And Dominique was very much a woman.

"I take it you approve of my swimsuit selection," she said, her arms going around his neck.

His trembling hands braced themselves on her trim waist to keep her from coming any closer. "Like I once said, I'll apologize early."

She smiled, a siren's smile. "Good. Then I'm glad I bought it yesterday."

"Yesterday," he echoed.

"The frame shop in Arlington was next door to a swim shop."

"So you decided to punish me for my rudeness the first time we met by getting a suit to give me a coronary, huh?" he teased.

Her regard grew serious. "I did buy it with you in mind, but not as punishment."

The significance of her statement sunk into Trent. "You wanted to please me."

"Yes."

The answer was so simple yet carried such a wealth of meaning behind it that Trent felt humbled and proud and scared all at once. Gently he enfolded her in his arms. "You're one special lady. I'll never abuse your trust."

"I think I realized that even before I bought the suit." Her cheek nuzzled his wide, bare chest that was sprinkled with black hair. "Janice was right. You are something in swim trunks."

"Stop that." He set her away, then grabbed her by the hand and started toward the pool. "We're going swimming."

Her laugh was sultry and bold. "Why, Trent, I do believe you're afraid of me sometimes."

He stopped so fast she almost bumped into him. "No I'm not," he said and dove into the pool. Emerging several feet away he said, "It's all the time."

A wide grin on her face, she dove in the pool after him.

They spent the afternoon playing in the pool and lounging, and when hunger and the encroaching shadows of darkness drove them inside they went to Janice's well-stocked kitchen. While Trent slowly chopped and diced his way through making a mixed green salad, Dominique prepared boneless chicken breasts to grill.

"You want me to do anything else?" Trent asked, dumping everything to a clear glass bowl.

Dominique glanced at the haphazard way he had thrown things together and smiled. It would taste the same. "No. I'll do the rest."

Trent walked over to the stove watching her every movement. "Your mother teach you how to cook?"

Dominique laughed before she could help herself. "Until recently, my mother couldn't cook an egg."

Frowning, Trent folded his arms across his shirted chest. "Then who did the cooking?"

Hearing the wonderment in his voice, she glanced up, ready to tell him about the cook. Then she remembered that Dominique Falcon had a cook, but Dominique Everette did not. Her gaze went back to the broccoli. "We managed."

Trent's arms went around her waist. "Every woman can't cook. From what I've heard, sounds like you and your parents are close. That what counts."

He was comforting her. His thoughtfulness never ceased to touch her. She wanted so much to not have any secrets between them, but she didn't want to take a chance of disturbing the delicate balance of their relationship. Then, too, she liked being liked for herself and not the Falcon name.

"Yes. That what counts." She turned in his arms. "I'm going to take a shower."

He made a face. "I don't suppose it would do me any more good to ask to wash your back than it did when I asked you when we got back earlier."

Dominique regarded his disgruntled expression with a smile. "No."

"Thought not." He kissed her on the cheek. "One of these days you're going to say yes."

She quivered inside. "There is that distinct possibility."

"I love it when you talk dirty to me." Grinning, he went to the kitchen door. "If you change your mind I'm only a phone call away."

"Be back to eat in ten minutes. I don't want to reheat the food."

"I'll be back in six, and maybe we can use the other four minutes to heat each other up." The door closed behind him.

Dominique didn't waste time. Quickly sliding the meat under the grill she checked the broccoli and rice, then headed for the shower. She wanted Trent so much she was trembling inside and she was tired of fighting it. Somehow she'd make him understand later the reason for not disclosing her identity.

Tossing off her cover-up, she hooked her thumbs in her spandex bikini bottoms. Maybe if they were lucky they'd have five minutes.

* * *

Trent made it back in five minutes, but Janice and Paul had returned in four from their date. The only reason Trent managed to greet them cordially was the look of disappointment on Dominique's face when she met him at the back door wearing an off the shoulder, hot pink, knit top and skintight black jeans. Somehow he knew she had purchased the top at the same time she purchased the swimsuit.

He let his gaze speak his approval. She flushed, but didn't look away.

"Dominique may rival you as the best cook in Texas, Janice," he said easily.

"According to Dominique you haven't eaten," Janice said from her seat at the round oak table.

Trent stared down at Dominique's. "A man doesn't always have to taste something to know it's going to be good."

"Trent," Dominique admonished, but she was smiling. "For that you have to serve yourself."

"Don't mind at all," he said, his eyes conveying a wealth of meaning.

Blushing, she turned away and asked Janice about the mutual friends she and Paul had gone to visit that afternoon. All the time Dominique was aware of Trent, and wished they could be alone.

It was not to be.

Janice and Paul sat with them while they ate, then remained as Trent and Dominique cleaned up the kitchen. Long before then, Dominique and Trent had begun giving each other covert looks.

Janice, usually talkative and smiling, sat grim-faced and silent. Paul, who had been charming and a bit of a tease at his restaurant, had retreated behind a troubled expression. He sat arrow straight in his chair, sneaking glances at Janice which she steadfastly refused to acknowledge.

Finally, Dominique had had enough. "Janice, there's a button off the suit I plan to wear tomorrow. Do you have a needle and thread?"

If Dominique had any doubt about there being a problem it vanished when Janice almost jumped up from the chair. "I'll get it for you."

Once in Janice's bedroom, Dominique asked, "What's the matter? Did he make a move on you?"

Janice's lower lip began to tremble.

Dominique saw red, and whirled toward the bedroom door.

Janice's hand on her arm stopped her. "Please wait."

"No man is going to treat you badly again," Dominique said fiercely.

Janice shook her head. "You don't understand. It isn't that he kissed me. It's that . . . that he called me Lilly. Lilly is the wife he lost fifteen years ago."

"Oh, Janice," Dominique said, pulling the other woman into her arms. She came easily.

"I just can't seem to get it right. First Wayne dumped me for someone younger, then Paul uses me for a stand-in for his dead wife." She sniffed. "I guess that says a lot about me."

Dominique set Janice away from her. "It says you're a goodhearted, loving woman. It's not your fault Wayne was trying to hang on to his youth, and Paul his past. If they didn't value you for the woman you are, it's their loss."

Janice stared at Dominique, her tears abating. "You've finally let go of the past."

"You can't look to the future without letting go," Dominique answered firmly. "I'm just beginning to see that."

"Trent helped, didn't he?"

"Yes."

"I'm glad." She touched Dominique's cheek. "Do you mind saying goodnight to Paul and Trent for me?"

"No. Can I bring you anything?" she said, her own eyes starting to tear. She'd never seen Janice look so desolate, so lost.

"Nothing. I'll say goodnight to you, too."

Squeezing her hands, Dominique closed the bedroom door and went back to the kitchen. She was ready to flay Paul alive until she saw the anxiety in his face as he came to his feet, his gaze going beyond her to an empty room.

"Where's Janice?"

She didn't remember his voice being that shaky. "She asked me to say goodnight to you."

For a moment he stared at Dominique as if he didn't understand what she had said, then he plopped back down in his seat. "I messed up."

The utter desolation in his words so closely echoed those in Janice's that Dominique felt tears sting her eyes again, but this time there was also anger. "You should have thought about that before you called her your dead wife's name."

"What?" His graying head came up sharply.

"You don't kiss a woman and call her by your dead wife's name," she repeated.

"I didn't," he defended, surging to his feet.

"You called her Lilly," Dominique said, her anger mounting when he shut his eyes.

"I think you'd better go," Trent said, his voice cold as he came to stand by Dominique.

Slowly Paul's eyes came open. "Lilly was my wife's first name, but I called her by her middle name—Ann."

"That's worse," Dominique riled. "At least she could

understand why you called her by your wife's name. Please leave."

Paul didn't move. His shaky hand ran over his head. "Please, can I speak with her? She misunderstood me."

Dominique crossed her arms and glared at the man. "A likely story."

"When I called her Lily, I didn't mean the name, I meant the flower. Janice has an innocent, pure quality like the flower. The Song of Solomon is my favorite book of the Bible. She is like a lily to me, with all its fragility and its uncompromising strength," he said passionately. "I called her my lily. My deceased wife was a wonderful woman, the mother of my children. I mourned her. But there is no way I'd confuse her with Janice."

Dominique's arms slowly uncrossed. She didn't know what to say.

"First door on the right," Trent told him.

"Thank you," Paul said.

Dominique placed her hand on Paul's jacketed arm as he started past her. "I hope for her sake you're telling the truth. You'd better hope for yours that you are."

His gaze didn't waver. "I am." Dominique's fingers slid from the fine gray wool. He continued out of the room.

She was still watching Paul when Trent's arms curved around her waist from behind, bringing her body against his. He placed his chin on top of her head. "I believe him, Dominique."

Her arms circled his. She leaned back against him. She couldn't see Janice's bedroom door, but she heard Paul's knock. "Why does caring for someone have to hurt?"

"It doesn't always."

"Tell that to Janice," Dominique said. "Or to me."

He turned her in his arms and stared down into her troubled eyes. "One of my foster parents' grandmother lived on a farm. We went there one summer to pick blueberries. Grandma Hawkins always said the sweetest berries were always deeper into the briar, and it stung like the dickens getting them, but one taste of the blueberry cobbler and you'd forget all the hurt you had to go through."

"Dominique. Trent."

They pivoted at the sound of Janice's soft voice. She was standing by Paul, his arm around her waist.

Janice's lipstick was smeared. Paul wore a smile. "I—" she began.

"I was just going over to Trent's," Dominique interrupted. "He was telling me about blueberry cobbler, and I want some."

Trent grabbed Dominique by the arm and headed for the back door. "Makes me hungry just thinking about it. I'll make sure she gets back safely. Goodnight Janice, Paul."

"Wait." Dominique opened the refrigerator door and pulled out the bottle of champagne Trent had given her. "Champagne and blueberries sounds like a natural combination to me."

"A natural," Trent agreed.

Giggling, Dominique followed. She was still laughing when Trent opened the door to his house and pulled her into his arms and silenced her with his lips.

Chapter Twelve

"What do you want to do first?" Trent asked on lifting his head.

Dominique's eyes widened in surprise. She had expected him to take her straight to bed.

"Since you don't seem to have a preference, maybe we should drink that champagne. Hunting for berries, as I remember, can make a person thirsty." Picking her up in his arms, he started toward the kitchen.

One arm hooked around his neck, her other hand holding the bottle of champagne, she stared up into his face with growing confusion. "Trent?"

"Don't worry. I won't be selfish and take all the berries for myself." He stared at her with dark, hungry eyes as he sat her on the white tile counter. "You trust me not to do that, don't you?"

She finally understood. Trent wasn't going to jump on her and take, thinking only of himself. He valued her. Was there ever a man who understood her more? "Yes," the word trembled over her lips as she drew the cold bottle of champagne against her.

"I'll get the glasses."

"As much as we've jostled it you'd better get the mop while you're at it," she called, trying to match his mood.

"Ye of little faith," he said, opening a drawer for a corkscrew, then reaching into the glass-fronted blue cabinets and removing two wineglasses. "Besides, I've been curious about something."

"What?" she asked, releasing the bottle to him.

"How champagne would taste on your skin."

Dominique was extremely glad she was sitting. Her body seemed to go all soft inside. "Trent." She wanted to kiss him again, taste him.

"Champagne first."

Dominique barely managed to nod. They both knew what would come before the night was over.

The cork came out with a pop. Wine fizzled and foamed over the sides. Trent regarded the small amount of wine on the counter with a frown. "Maybe I should have shaken it again?"

Dominique accepted the long-stemmed glass, pleased her fingers trembled only slightly. "There's always next time."

His dark brown eyes seemed to narrow. "I'll hold you to that."

She swallowed, then moistened her dry lips. "What should we drink to?"

"To second chances and new beginnings." His glass clinked against hers.

"Second chances and new beginnings." She drank the wine, her gaze unable to leave his.

Slowly he took the glass from her hand and stepped

between her legs and framed her face with hands that trembled. "I look at you and ache all over."

Her hands covered his, her gaze steady and sure. "I feel the same way and I'm tired of fighting it." Her lips gently touched his. "I want to be here with you. Only you."

A fierce pleasure ripped through Trent. His forehead touched hers. "Despite what I said, I sometimes doubted."

She exerted enough pressure to lift his head until their eyes met. "Now that you've shamelessly worn down my resistance, I hope you'll live up to the promises you made each time you looked at me the way you're now looking at me."

"How am I looking at you?" he asked, his voice rough and strained.

"As if you could eat me with a spoon and lick your lips afterward," she said, her voice shaky.

"That about covers it." His lips met hers, warm and gentle, then with increased hunger. Dominique matched his hunger and tested the limits of his control.

He had intended to go slowly, make the night one they'd both remember and cherish. As soon as his tongue slipped into the dark interior of Dominique's mouth and her tongue swirled around his, he knew he had overestimated himself and underestimated her.

He didn't waste time thinking about his miscalculations. He just tightened his hold and enjoyed his downfall.

Need trampled through her. She strained to be closer. Trent helped by sliding her hips forward. His blunt arousal brushed teasingly against the notch of her thighs.

So close and yet too far.

His hands swept up her sides, closing over her breasts. His thumb flicked once, twice, across her nipple. She arched, pressing closer to the sweet pain. It was all the encouragement he needed. Lifting his head for an instant, he grabbed her top and jerked it up over her head.

He caught a glimpse of a wisp of pink, lacy perfection masquerading as a bra just before his teeth closed over her dusky brown nipple and tugged. A cry of pleasure broke over her lips.

She heard him murmur something about berries, but couldn't understand. She had only a heartbeat to wonder why, since her hearing was so acute. His mouth closed over the other nipple, his tongue sliding across the turgid point, and her thoughts scattered.

Unconsciously, her hands wrapped around his head, anchoring him in place. The sensation was exquisite.

She wanted to kiss him the same way. She wanted him to feel the same sharp urgency, so intense it was almost painful but filled with so much pleasure she was light-headed.

Releasing him, she jerked his shirt out of his jeans. Unsteady fingers fumbled the buttons free. Unerringly, her lips found his nipple buried in the soft texture of his chest hair.

Trent groaned.

Dominique smiled like a well-fed cat. She suddenly realized what he meant about berries.

"No more." Trent pulled her head up and saw the pleasure in her face from giving him pleasure, and his knees almost buckled.

"Unless things have changed in eight years, there's a lot more."

Shock went through him at her words, and then another deeper, more complex emotion he couldn't define. He felt weak and strong, the seducer and the protector. "You're everything I've ever wanted in a woman, and so much more." Sweeping her up in his arms, he grabbed the bottle of champagne and headed for the master bedroom at the back of the house.

The spacious room lay in semi-darkness, but he had no difficulty finding the king-size bed. Setting the champagne on the nightstand, he pulled back the multicolored, Kente-inspired bedspread, then tenderly placed her on the cool, black cotton sheets. "Stay here."

Dominique would have laughed if she'd had enough breath. Her knees wouldn't support her even if she had any inclination to leave. She didn't.

The snap of his jeans coming undone sounded overly loud in the charged atmosphere, as did the rustle of the denim material sliding down his legs. Her calming heart hitched.

Somewhere in the shadowed room she heard the faint hiss of a match. By the time Trent finished lighting the candles on the six arm, double candelabras on the mahogany mantel, her heart was racing. Faint whiffs of cinnamon drifted out to her. Golden embers from the gas logs glowed in the open, polished, brick fireplace.

She was being seduced. The fact that he didn't have to go to such measures endeared him to her more.

Crossing the room, Trent turned down the thermostat and shut the door. Gaslight and candlelight, the only illuminations, played over his conditioned muscles and created shadows on his handsome face and lean body.

Silently he came to her, naked and majestic. She trembled at the sight of him, but not from fear.

A knee dug into the mattress beside her, and his hands cupped her face again. "I knew you'd look even more beautiful with candlelight dancing on your skin."

A long, lean finger brushed across her lip, the curve of her jaw, then curved until reaching her nipple. She trembled. "I've imagined how you'd taste, but all my fantasies and speculations were pitifully inadequate. It's not just the taste, it's how you make me feel when my mouth is on you and I hear your cries of pleasure, and know they're just for me." His head bent, taking the pebbly point into his mouth.

A shudder went through Dominique. Her body went liquid. Before she knew it she was minus her jeans and panties and Trent's powerful body was crouched over hers. In a moment of panic a distant memory pricked up, but before she could respond to the fear his hand swept up her bare leg to the center of her body. A finger dipped inside.

A ragged moan of pleasure, not fear, slipped over her lips.

"I knew the fire was there. Waiting to be stoked, waiting to be found."

He unhooked the front fasteners of her bra, his hands covering the silky firmness of her breasts, kneading the resilient flesh. His mouth came back to hers, his tongue dipping, twirling, in her mouth as his lower body touched hers maddeningly.

The ravenous and deeply erotic kiss stole what little control Dominique had left. Trent was right about the fire, only it was raging in one spot. She whimpered, twisting on the bed, her arms straining to bring him closer.

His mouth left hers again. She moaned her protest, then gasped in shocked pleasure as he kissed her in the most intimate of places. She was helpless to fight the tightening of her body being pushed over the edge. When it came she cried out Trent's name in helpless surrender.

He was there.

Gathering her still trembling body in his arms, he slid into her moist warmth, only to retreat and return again. His body set up a relentless rhythm that she matched and followed effortlessly. This time, when completion came they were together.

Rolling to his side, Trent took Dominique with him, his breathing labored. He had never known making love could be so explosive or satisfying. Never had he experienced anything like it. Somehow he sensed he never would with another woman. Dominique had challenged and broken rules he had established to live by. Tonight she had done it again.

Perhaps because he had had to share a bed until he was in his teens he liked sleeping alone, and he liked doing it in spacious comfort. His gaze returned to the woman in his arms, her black hair spilling over his pillow, her bare shoulders. His arms tightened. He couldn't imagine leaving her.

Warm lips pressed a kiss to her lips. "You're all right?"

Her eyelids fluttered open to reveal languid black eyes. "Wonderful."

"Good." He reached for the bottle of champagne and splashed a dab over her navel. "Time for dessert."

Dominique stretched luxuriously in Trent's large bed early the next morning, then hastily drew her bare arms back beneath the covers. The bedroom was still chilly. Trent had forgotten to turn the thermostat back up until a couple of hours ago.

Her pleased smile broadened. It wasn't that he had forgotten. He had been busy with other things. All of them fantastic.

She thought she knew her body, knew about sexual pleasure, but with a mixture of tenderness and aggression Trent had shown her much more. She had absolutely no desire to be anyplace except where she was.

Content for the first time in years, she smiled and snuggled against Trent's muscled warmth. His arm came around her waist dragging her closer.

He spoke without lifting his head, "If you want to go jogging, I'll go with you."

"I'd rather go riding."

His head came up, a frown on his face until she threw one long leg over his waist. His eyes darkened to tiny points of desire. Catching her by the waist he shifted, allowing her to straddle him.

She captured the pulsating warmth of his manhood and guided him. Eyes closed, she savored the exquisite pleasure of them being joined inch by incredible inch.

"Look at me."

Her eyelids fluttered opened. What she saw in the depth of his gaze filled her in an entirely different way. She wanted to tell him, but no words came. She knew a way.

Her body moved against his, with his. Her knees locked at his sides, felt the power and the passion of his body beneath her, felt her own power as a shudder ripped through him. Her hands braced against his chest, she took them to the point of no return.

She collapsed on his chest. His hand stroked the damp, smooth curve of her back to the roundness of her hips.

"Lady, what you do to me," he said, when he had enough breath to do so.

Satisfaction curled through Dominique. "I'm glad, because you've given so much to me." She felt him smile. "I didn't mean *that.*"

Chuckling, he put his arms around her and she found herself hoisted in his arms. He started to the shower. "I told you I love it when you talk dirty to me."

* * *

Dominique was nervous. Janice would surely be up by seven-thirty, and once she saw Dominique wearing the same clothes she'd know. Then, there was another problem. Her hand lifted to her damp, tangled hair.

"It really looks fine," Trent said, brushing his hand across her head.

Dominique knew her hair was a tangled mess. She didn't regret helping to get it that way, but she did regret having to face her godmother.

"Come on," Trent said, tugging her hand.

"Maybe I should go in alone," she suggested, biting her lip.

"No deal. We're in this together. Janice is not going to crucify you." Stopping, he stared down into her troubled face, then took her into his arms. "It will be all right."

"I hope so."

"Have I let you down yet?"

Raising her head, she quirked an eyebrow. "That, I believe, is the reason I'm in the predicament I'm in."

"I told you I aim to please." Kissing her on the nose, he continued the short distance to the door and knocked.

"Come in," called Janice.

Squeezing Dominique's hand, Trent opened the door and curved his arm around her waist so they walked through the door together. "Good morning, Janice."

"Morning, Janice," Dominique greeted slowly.

Janice glanced up from behind the refrigerator door. "Good morning. Breakfast is almost ready."

"Is there anything I can do?" Dominique offered, breathing easier since her godmother didn't look at her any differently.

"If you can handle the French toast, Trent can set the table," Janice said, closing the refrigerator door and placing a package of breakfast ham on the counter.

Both jumped to do as she asked. Soon they were all sitting at the table. After Janice had given the blessing, she looked at Trent and said, "I guess we'll be seeing more of you."

Dominique almost choked on her toast. Her gaze went to Trent, and knew they were both thinking of the term literally.

Clearing his throat he answered, "Yes. I hope that'll be all right with you?"

Janice turned to Dominique. "You're sure?"

"I'm sure," she said, feeling Trent's approving gaze on her.

Janice picked up her coffee cup. "Looks like I'd better double up on the groceries."

"Hey, I don't eat that much," Trent protested.

"No, but you and Paul will together," she told him.

"You're sure?" Dominique asked.

Janice set her cup down before answering. "The only thing I'm sure of is that I'm not sure of anything."

"Sounds like me after I met Dominique," Trent said thoughtfully.

"And look how that turned out," Janice commented.

Dominique blushed.

Trent grinned.

She wanted to throw her toast at him. Instead, she stood. "I need to get to the studio. I have a lot to do before Samuel Jacobs and his family arrive."

"Give Samuel and his wife my best," Trent told her.

"I will." Dominique went to her room with a smile on her face. Life was definitely on an upswing.

* * *

Samuel Jacobs's grandson, Michael, was a rascal. But a cute rascal. It was obvious five minutes after he came into Dominique's studio already dressed in his new gray, striped overalls that his grandparents doted on him. It was just as obvious that his mother made sure her son knew she was in charge.

His sister, Gia, was a chubby five-year-old with a sunny disposition and a giggly laugh that was infectious. Dominique looked at the beautiful little girl in the snug fitting purple tutu, tiara and rouged cheeks, and knew the outfit was all wrong.

"Mrs. Marshall, may I see you a moment, please?"

"Of course." Frowning, the mother followed.

Dominique dug her hands into the front pockets of her navy trousers. This wasn't going to be easy.

Dominique's mother, Felicia, had taught her all about the fierceness of a mother's love. Dominique didn't think Mrs. Marshall was any different. One wrong word and she would be out the door.

Dissatisfied customers, especially those as influential as the Lloyds, could ruin her business. But she had to take the chance.

"I don't think the costume is right for Gia. She has too much energy."

Mrs. Marshall's lips tightened. "What do you suggest?"

Dominique took a deep breath and plunged in. "The classic setting for such a photograph would suggest serenity. That's not Gia. She bubbles over with life. I want to show that. I'd like her to come back in a long, white summer dress and small white straw hat, and shoot her in front of a background of wildflowers with the sun setting in the distance, with a kite in her hand."

The mother emitted a startled outcry—"Oh!"

"What is it, Carolyn?" asked Mrs. Jacobs.

Dominique thought, *Here it comes,* but held her ground. If she were going to be a photographer she had to do it without compromising her principles.

"Ms. Everette just suggested another pose for Gia instead of the ballet costume, and I agree with her," Mrs. Marshall said. She turned to her daughter. "You get to fly a kite, Sweetie."

Gia smiled broadly, then glanced at the ceiling. "Will it fly in here?"

Mrs. Marshall faced Dominique. "I'm sure Ms. Everette will think of something. Isn't that right?"

"You just leave everything to me."

How do you get yourself into these things? Dominique thought as she tried to figure out a way to suspend the kite with the illusion of the wind tugging at it in the studio. A fan might work if it were far enough awa—"

The buzzer sounded. She glanced up. Her face broke into a wide smile. Pressing the buzzer for admittance, she hurried to meet Trent halfway. Seconds later she was in his arms, his lips on hers.

He smiled down into her upturned face. "Now, that's what I call a welcome."

"I suppose you just happened to be passing by?" she teased, her fingers twined around the back of his neck.

"No, I missed you and I didn't want to wait until tonight to see you," he told her frankly. "If not for all this glass, I'd show you exactly how much."

Her heart sped up. "I'd let you, too."

"You're making it awfully difficult for me to behave."

She grinned. "I could say the same thing about you."

"You'd better." He kissed her on the nose. "I have a surprise for you tonight."

"What?"

"If I told you—"

"It wouldn't be a surprise," she finished with a pout.

He laughed and hugged her to him. "I love teasing you."

I love you. The words popped into Dominique's head and almost tumbled over her lips.

"Honey, what's wrong?" he asked, staring down into her troubled face. "You're trembling."

"I—" She couldn't tell him. That would mean the ultimate in being vulnerable. With an effort she brought a smile to her lips. "I guess I'm a little tired."

"My fault. You'll get a good night's sleep tonight," he promised.

She pulled her arms down. She tried to tell herself that she should be pleased that he was being thoughtful again, but somehow she felt abandoned. "I should get back to work."

His hands on her waist held her in place. His gaze intent, he said, "If this is going to work we have to be honest with each other."

Some secrets she wasn't ready to divulge, but he was right. "I guess I didn't think you'd get tired of me so soon." She wasn't prepared for the anger that flashed across his face or to find herself off the floor and staring into his blazing eyes.

"Tired of you? What gave you such a crazy idea?"

She would have been indignant if his anger hadn't stunned her. "You—you said I'd get a good night's sleep."

"That's right. So we'd better get to bed early. Any objections?"

She shook her head. "None."

"Good." He set her on her feet. "Then I trust there won't be a reason to have this conversation again."

"I'm sorry," she said. "I just . . ." Her voice trailed off. She glanced away.

A lean, hard finger brought her head back around. "Don't start doubting me or yourself. And remember, whatever it is we talk about it, no jumping to conclusions. All we have to do is be honest with each other, and things will be fine."

She shifted restlessly. "Things aren't as simple for some of us," she told him while thinking of her real identity, her love.

"They can be if you let them."

"Perhaps," she said evasively.

"Sounds as if you need convincing." He kissed her hard on the lips, then went to the door. "It's a good thing I enjoy a challenge."

Dominique watched his truck pull away from the curb, her thoughts troubled. He might enjoy a challenge, but he detested dishonesty. Somehow she had to find a way to tell him about her identity. The longer she waited, the harder it was going to be for both of them.

Trent deserved total honesty. She could give him nothing less. Somehow she'd make him understand she hadn't intentionally deceived him, that she had simply been trying to make it on her own.

Tonight. She'd tell him tonight. Her mind made up, she turned toward her desk.

The buzzer sounded. She glanced around. Her hand, already reaching for the control, froze.

Standing outside the glass door were Isaac and three other male teenagers, including Jessie. Isaac twisted the doorknob, pounded on the glass. When the door didn't open, the teenagers began making lewd, suggestive motions with their bodies and hands while mouthing the foul words.

Disgusted, she jerked up the phone. They should be in school instead of bothering her. She was calling the police.

Her gaze switching from the youths to the phone, she punched in 9, then 1, then 1. Frantically pointing to her, three of the boys ran out of sight, leaving Isaac to make one last hand gesture before following.

Moments later a fast moving, battered, red Camaro sped past the front of the studio with Isaac and another teenagers hanging out of the windows, yelling what she was sure were obscenities. Her hand trembling, she dropped the receiver back into place.

What could she tell the police? That some teenagers had made suggestive gestures and then run? Hardly enough to warrant the call.

Yet, if Trent found out about the incident there was no telling what he might do. It wasn't worth the possibility of his getting into trouble with the police. She was safe inside the studio, and she always left before dark. She wasn't worried about them coming back. They had fled too quickly when she had picked up the phone. Cowards, all of them.

Rounding her desk, she sat down and wondered how they had found her, then decided it didn't matter. Determined to forget them, she went back to working on the photo shoot for Gia.

Trent was smiling broadly when he entered his outer office. With a wave to Anita, who was on the phone, he went to his private office and sat behind his desk. Scooting his chair closer, he picked up the ballpoint pen he had left on top of the bid proposal earlier.

Seconds ticked away. The pen remained immobile. His mind was three point, seven miles away in Deep Ellum, more specifically on Dominique Everette.

By nature, he wasn't an impulsive person. Yet, he had wanted to see her and had simply given into the urge to do so. He leaned back in his chair and freely admitted he hadn't been a lot of things before he met Dominique. He didn't mind the new Trent one bit. He couldn't remember being happier.

In his mind he replayed the happy expression on Dominique's beautiful face when she saw him, the utterly beguiling taste of her lips, the way her body melted against him. He didn't see how it could get any better than this.

Every moment with her was fantastic. And when he wasn't with her, he wanted to be. He loved everything about her.

He loved her.

The realization didn't shock him. Since he had first seen her, he had been falling. He'd gone to the mat and stayed there when she came over to comfort him after his confrontation with Isaac. However, he didn't think she was ready to hear the words.

Her jumping to conclusions when he mentioned letting her get a good night's sleep was evidence that she remained unsure about their relationship. She wouldn't for long. He was going to show her in every possible way that they had a future together. He was used to working hard for what he wanted, and Dominique Everette was definitely at the top of his want list.

This time things were going to turn out differently. This time he didn't have to worry about deceit and dishonesty from the woman he loved. This time his second chance at happiness was just the beginning.

Chapter Thirteen

Dominique had planned to tell Trent the moment she saw him. Her plans were altered when he came over after six that evening and insisted she come with him at once. Janice, planning to go out later with Paul to a movie, waved them off with a smile.

Dominique had gone willingly, prepared to explain everything to him, until he showed her her first surprise in his bedroom. Two dozen pink and white roses sat in a delicately etched, crystal vase on the dresser. Beside the flowers were a sterling silver comb and brush. Her unsteady hand picked up the comb, then the brush.

"There's another present over there."

A long, pink, silk robe lay on the bed. Beside it was a pair of matching slippers.

"There's one more." Tugging her hand, he took her into the large bathroom that held an oversized sunken tub and a glass enclosed shower, then pointed to the top of the black marbled vanity.

A dryer. A lump formed in her throat. She turned to him, the brush still clutched to her chest.

"I knew you were upset this morning about your hair. I hope you don't mind."

"Mind?" Her arms went around his neck. She gazed up at him. "Thank you. Your thoughtfulness always makes me feel special."

"You *are* special." His arms circled her waist. "But I benefit, too. We can make love in the shower or the tub and neither of us has to worry about your hair."

"T—Trent." His name trembled on her lips. A familiar heat began to build inside her.

His hands lifted and began unbuttoning her white blouse. "What do you say we test the dryer? You never know when you might get a dud."

Placing the brush on the vanity, she smiled up at him, her hand closing around his masculinity. "A problem you don't have."

He nipped her on the ear. "And aren't you pleased?"

"Very."

His fingers made short work of her cotton blouse and lacy bra. "Then I know you'll be happy about something else."

She was almost as quick with his shirt. "What?"

He reached for the button on her slacks. "Ice cream."

Her hands paused on the snap of his jeans. "Ice cream?"

He grinned wickedly. "Trust me."

For a long, satisfying time Dominique could barely lift her eyelashes. She did, though, just enough to see Trent's slumbering face inches from hers on the pillow they shared. She felt the sheet on her and knew he had pulled it over them. She hadn't had the strength.

She should have known when he said "Trust me" with a gleam in his eyes that he was going to do things to her body that still made her blush. Her lashes closed as she remembered doing similar things—and enjoying every sensual, erotic-filled moment.

She'd never think of ice cream in the same way again.

"I'm going to help with your hair as soon as I can sit up."

Dominique opened her eyes to find herself staring into Trent's dark gaze. She loved him more with each passing moment. Somehow she found the strength to move enough to touch his face with her fingertips. "We need to talk."

"Later." His mouth found hers again and once again she was taken to a place only Trent could take her. By the time he joined her, she had ceased to think.

The next morning Dominique didn't think about telling Trent until she was halfway to work. She'd just have to tell him that evening. When she arrived home Janice put her to work helping prepare for the neighborhood block party in their backyard. During the laughter-filled gathering, she was too busy meeting the mostly elderly neighbors and helping Janice and the other ladies make sure they didn't run out of food or drink to think of much else.

It was almost eleven when the last couple left. Trent had taken her back to his house and straight to bed. The following night they double-dated with Janice and Paul and went to a dinner show at the Venetian Room in the Fairmont Hotel. This time she took Trent straight to bed. She really planned to talk with him when she arrived home Thursday, but they went to watch The Tigers practice and show them their pictures. They stayed at home Friday night, but by then her courage had decreased dramatically. She didn't want to chance ruining their relationship.

Her days were filled with doing a job she loved: her nights in the arms of a man she loved. She had waited so long for the former and hadn't known how much she wanted the latter until Trent had walked into her life.

As days turned into weeks, she knew she had no choice. Her family was becoming suspicious, since she was gone so much at night. Dominique expected them to pay her a visit any day. Before that happened, she had to tell Trent.

"A penny for your thoughts?" Trent said beside her one night in bed, their heads on the same pillow.

Her fingertips grazed his lips, traced his dark brow. "I guess it's time I told you."

Frowning, his hand caught hers. He kissed her palm. "What is it, Honey?"

"I know you think of everything in black and white with no shades of gray, but that isn't always the case with some of us," she said carefully.

"Is this about your marriage?"

"No. You banished LaSalle completely," she told him truthfully. "I didn't think that was possible before I met you."

"Then this isn't about another man?"

"This is about us. If . . . if afterwards you still want there to be an us."

His arms closed tightly around her, dragging her to him. "Don't ever scare me like that again. You had me thinking you were going to leave me."

"You may want me to after I've finished."

He sat her away from him, his gaze searching. "This sounds serious."

"It is."

"I'm listening."

She bit her lower lip. "I think we should get dressed first."

His hands tightened for a split second, then opened. "You can get dressed, but you're not leaving me."

She had to touch him one last time. She laid her hand on his chest. "That will be up to you." She turned away from him, gathered up her clothes, and dressed in silence.

Finished, she went down the hallway and perched on the edge of the chair framing the window in the living room. It wasn't lost on either of them that the seat was only a few feet from the door.

Trent stared at her choice of seats, then pulled the matching chair around her, effectively blocking her escape, and sat down. He didn't know what was going on, but she was not running away from him. There was another surprise he intended to give her tonight, and nothing she said was going to change that.

"Whenever you're ready."

Dominique clasped her hands together. Nothing had been this hard, not even telling Daniel about the horrors LaSalle had put her through.

"If you want to, we can forget this, do your hair, then have the dinner I picked up on my way home," he suggested. "It's Chinese."

She didn't even think of taking his offer. It was now or never. She moistened her dry lips. "Janice was right about a second chance. I needed one desperately. I needed to find something that brought peace and permanence. I had been looking and wandering for eight years."

"Since your divorce?" he asked.

"Yes. It . . . it wasn't pleasant."

He came out of his seat to kneel in front of her. His

hands gripped hers. "You don't have to tell me anything more about that. It isn't hard to imagine what happened when you were tied up."

Shame went through her. She tried to tug her hands free. It was impossible.

"Listen, Dominique. You have nothing to be ashamed of. Don't you think I felt you tense sometimes when I touched you? If that bastard hadn't been dead, he would be now," Trent said fiercely. "But you're past that now. In the past weeks we've been as intimate as a man and woman can get, and you were with me all the way. He's behind you. You're independent and strong. You're free."

"Now." she said, continuing slowly, "but when I came to Dallas all I had were dreams. I was running from who I am, and trying to prove to the world I was as talented as anyone in my family." Her hands clutched his. "To the people who loved me it didn't matter, and I shouldn't have let others influence me into thinking it did."

"He made you think it did," Trent told her.

"Yes. During the nine months of our marriage my best was never good enough, and afterward I was never quite as sure of myself."

"It's over. You're stronger now. You can accomplish anything you want."

She pulled her hands free. "I know that now, but it took caring about you, being around you, to make me realize that. I don't regret how I handled things. I regret thinking it was the only way."

"What are you talking about?"

"I wanted to make it on my own as a portrait photographer. I didn't want another failure in my life," she told him tightly. "I wanted no one to be able to say I had used my family connections, as they did in Paris."

"Paris?" He straightened. "I thought you modeled after high school."

"I did, then off and on since then," she told him watching him stand and move back a step. So it had begun already.

"So when did you start taking pictures?" he asked.

"Two years ago we were on location for a fashion shoot for a European magazine at a small fishing village, and the photographer's assistant became ill. I was finished for the day so I volunteered to help. Looking through the lens instead of being on the other side opened a whole new world. Most photographers start very young, but I was determined."

"Apparently you learned well."

A chill went through her. His controlled words hadn't sounded like a compliment. "I like to think so. It was past time for me to find something I enjoyed, and was good at. I tried a couple of other business ventures, became bored, then sold out. In the meantime I wandered around the world."

"It takes money to do both."

She started to drag her hand through her hair, encountered the tangles, and put her hand in her lap. "Yes, it does. But I have money."

"How did you get it?" he asked, taking a step toward her.

"The old-fashioned way. I inherited it."

His brown eyes narrowed. "If you have money, why were you so worried about your business?"

"Because I want to succeed on my own," she reminded him. "For once in my life I want to stand and accomplish something on my own merits and know it's not because of my last name."

His hand brushed across his head. "Come on, Dominique. I keep up on African-Americans who are the movers and shakers in the business world, and I don't remember seeing Everette on the list."

"That's because my grandfather retired years ago. I'm sure the name Falcon was on the list."

He went still. "What did you say?"

She pushed to her feet. "Everette is my mother's maiden name. My given name is Dominique Nicole Falcon."

"What is Daniel Falcon to you, your cousin or something?"

"My brother."

Trent said one explicit word before turning away, then whipping back around so fast that she jumped. "You really had me going," he said, his face and voice hard. "You must have had a great time laughing at me trying to help you with your business. You can probably buy the entire building—no, make that the block—and not put a dent in your checkbook."

There was only one accusation she wanted to talk about. "I never laughed at you. I had given myself two years to succ—"

Dry laughter cut her off. "Two years! If you hadn't succeeded, what would you have done?" His hands lifted when she opened her mouth. "Don't tell me. I think I can guess the answer. Go back to wandering and being a part-time model and living a life most people can only dream about."

"When I first came here you might have been right," she told him frankly, and rushed on when his expression hardened. "That's not true anymore. I'm tired of moving from one place to the other. I want more out of life."

His temper flared higher. "So what was I? Your entertainment to keep you from being bored?"

"You know that isn't true!" she cried. "I care about you.

You're the first man I've made love to since I left my husband."

"So I'm supposed to be grateful for the privilege, is that it?" Cold eyes swept from her tousled head to her booted feet. "The sister of Daniel Falcon allowed herself to condescend to make love with a man whose income is pocket change to him."

"Don't you see? You just said it yourself. Before I told you who I was, I was Dominique. Once I did, I'm relegated to being Daniel Falcon's sister," she said fighting her own anger, fighting tears. "I love my brother, but I hate being in his shadow. I wanted to make it on my own, but I failed. If you hadn't stepped in to help, I'd still be looking for my first big customer."

"Yeah, good ol' Trent, being suckered in by another beautiful woman to help her business." He laughed bitterly. "I was so sure you were different, but you're worse than Margo. At least she had a real need. But you just used me."

Her own temper finally slipped free. "That's nonsense. I never asked for your help."

"You didn't have to ask. Most men would do anything to help you, and you know it."

Black eyes narrowed. "Yes, and you know what they expect in return."

His head snapped back. "That's not the reason I helped you, and you damn well know that," he yelled.

"Then you should damn well know the only reason I went to bed with you is that I care about you!" she shouted just as loudly.

"Not enough to be honest with me."

The fight went out of her. She reached for him. "I was afraid you wouldn't understand."

He pulled his arm away. "Oh, I understand perfectly. I don't want to hear any more."

"Why won't you listen?" she asked.

"I *did* listen. You should have listened to me." His voice had a final ring.

Fear made her tremble. "I thought you were so big on second chances. Don't you think I deserve one?"

Trent gazed into the depths of her eyes and knew if she didn't leave soon she wouldn't until he had compromised another principle and taken her on any terms. "Good-bye, Dominique. Tell Janice to stop buying extra groceries. I won't be coming over anymore."

Dominique shook her head, accepting defeat. "No, don't do that to her. I'll leave. There's a loft apartment next door to the studio."

"That area isn't safe at night," he flared.

She wanted to take comfort because he still worried about her, then she remembered he was a caring man. He cared about her, but he didn't love her, and he wasn't going to forgive her. "Good-bye, Trent." She stepped around him, opened the door, then closed it softly behind her.

Hearing the door close was like hearing the sound of his heart being ripped out. Dominique Falcon. Another rich, spoiled socialite had stuck it to him. How could he have been so stupid? At least he had found out before he had given her her surprise.

He stalked back to his bedroom and went straight to the fresh vase of roses. Pushing aside one tight bud, then another, he finally located the pink rose he sought.

Laying in the center of the perfect, open flower was a two-carat, flawless diamond ring in a heavy platinum band encrusted with gemstones. The ring was as unusual and as beautiful as the woman he had intended to give it to—a friendship ring that he had hoped in time would represent a deeper, more lasting commitment.

He scowled. Grabbing the ring, he opened the drawer and tossed it inside. The brush set followed. He whirled and picked up the robe, intending to trash it, but found himself clutching it instead. Sitting on the bed, he let his forehead fall into the palm of his hand.

He had never hurt this much in his life. His chest felt strangely tight; his throat ached. Why couldn't Dominique be who she'd pretended to be—a struggling photographer needing a second chance—instead of an incredibly wealthy woman who didn't need him?

And that was what tore at him. She didn't need him. There wasn't one single thing in the world he could give her that she couldn't get for herself.

Her wealthy and powerful family dated back centuries; he didn't even know who his mother was. Dominique could toss him aside just as easily and carelessly as his mother had.

The pressure on his chest increased.

He couldn't stay here. Standing, he tossed the robe onto the bench at the foot of the bed, grabbed his keys, and left the room. There was always paperwork at the offi—

A woman's scream pierced the night.

Less than a heartbeat later Trent knew it was Dominique. Terror ripped through him. Heart pounding, more frightened than he had ever been in his life, he raced to the front door and jerked it open.

What he saw sent raw fear coursing through him. He was off the porch and running all out toward Isaac, who was trying to drag the struggling Dominique into the open back door of a battered Camaro.

"Stay back, Old Man, or I'll cut the bitch," Isaac warned,

his eyes wild, his unsteady hand holding the handle of a six-inch knife to Dominique's throat.

Trent's blood went cold. His gaze briefly flickered to Dominique, trying to reassure her. Her gaze locked on his. She stopped struggling. 'Let her go. It's me you want.''

"Yeah, but you want her," Isaac sneered. "I've been watching you since the first night you spent together, waiting for this chance. I knew an old man like you couldn't keep going."

"Come on, Man, let's get out of here," yelled the driver. "The porch light across the street came on."

"Maybe you should let her go?" suggested an unsteady voice.

"Shut up, Jessie. I'm running this." Isaac took another step backward. Trent followed. "I told you to stay back, unless you want me to slash her pretty throat. You can have her back after I'm through with her."

"You'll have to kill me first."

"That could be arranged." Isaac thrust the knife out toward him.

Trent couldn't believe what happened next. Dominique thrust her left elbow sharply into Isaac's stomach, dropped, whirled, and grabbed his arm, spinning him around so that he was between her and the three teenagers in the car, then pushed his arm high up behind his back.

"Ow! Let go of my arm!"

"Drop the knife." Dominique didn't have to say it but once. Metal clattered to the sidewalk.

"Get this bit—ohhh!"

"I wouldn't say that word again if you want to use your arm again," Dominique warned, her voice steady.

A police siren sounded in the distance.

"I'm getting outta here," said the driver, reaching for the gearshift.

Trent moved, grabbing the young man through the open window and dragging him out of the car. With his other hand, Trent cut the motor and pocketed the keys. "I don't think so."

The passenger door abruptly swung open. Out jumped another teenager. He ran down the street without looking back. Less than fifty feet away he stumbled and fell when his baggy pants slid down around his knees.

By the time he managed to get up he was pinned by the high beam light of a police car. Another police vehicle came from the other direction. The wail of a third car grew louder.

"Dominique, are you all right? Did he hurt you?" Trent asked, keeping the teenager he'd subdued on the grass.

No answer.

"Dammit, be pissed at me tomorrow, but please turn around and tell me you're all right." he said, his voice ragged with fear.

A policeman and a policewoman jumped out of the second car and ran over, "What's going on here?"

"He tried to force her into that car with his friends," Trent explained, dragging his prisoner to his feet and handing the officer the car keys.

"He's lying," Isaac yelled.

"Turn them loose," ordered the slender black policewoman, her hair in microbraids.

"What?" Trent yelled.

"You heard me," said the officer.

Dominique released Isaac. The instant he was free, he swung at her with his fist. She blocked the blow and sent a quick jab to his nose with the heel of her hand.

He went down, rolling and cursing.

With a savage curse, Trent started for Isaac. The two

officers grabbed him, then were aided by another policeman who had arrived in the third patrol car.

"You see, they're both crazy. I just brought my cousin
over here and they went medieval on us," Isaac cried, his
words muffled from holding his hands over his bleeding
nose.

"That's a lie!" Trent yelled. "I heard Dominique scream
and came out, and you were trying to pull her into that
car."

"You saw what she did to me," Isaac said, moaning. "I
couldn't have dragged her unless she wanted to come.
Maybe she wanted a real man between the sheets."

Trent lunged for Isaac. The officers tightened their
holds.

"See, what did I tell you? I need a doctor," Isaac wailed.
"My cousin will tell you. Tell him Jessie. We were just
coming over for him to visit and try and get back on the
football team."

Jessie, in a black sweatshirt, oversized jeans, and a sideways baseball cap, eyes wide, was trembling as he got out
of the car. "I—I don't want to go to jail."

"Jessie, don't lie for him," Trent said. "You don't have
to go the same way as Isaac. I'll help you."

"Now he's trying to bribe my cousin," Isaac flared. "He
has money." The youth glanced around at the growing
crowd gathering on Trent's lawn and across the street.
"His neighbors will probably lie for him. We're just poor,
honest kids."

"Cut the crap, Isaac," said the policeman, who came
up with the other teenager who had tried to run. "I don't
know about the rest of these kids, but Isaac has a long rap
sheet. I arrested him myself for car theft when I worked
the Southwest Division."

"I've been going straight," Isaac whined.

Dominique stepped forward. "If you'll look on the curb by the car you'll find a knife with Isaac's fingerprints. And if that isn't enough to prove Trent told you the truth, I don't think I would have gotten this if I were willing."

She tilted her head to the side. Blood welled from a two-inch cut on the side of her neck.

Chapter Fourteen

Trent exploded in a cry of rage. Another policeman rushed to help with subduing him.

"Trent," Dominique said calmly. "If you're in jail, who's going to take me to the doctor?"

"Oh, Lord." He started toward her, then found himself unable to do so. He gazed at the police officers. "Please, let me go to her. I won't touch him."

The officers looked at the lone female officer, who had two stripes on her sleeve. She nodded.

As soon as Trent was free he rushed to Dominique, picked her up in his arms, and ran back to the house.

Several neighbors Dominique recognized from the block party followed—which proved to be for the best, Dominique realized, because Trent had completely lost it. An elderly woman whom Dominique remembered as Mrs. Garland, a retired nurse, finally got him to put her down on the sofa. When Dominique protested she might get blood on the white material, Trent picked her up again and hugged her so tight she had difficulty breathing.

Once again Mrs. Garland took control. She sent her husband for her first aid kid, then said, "Trent, I can't see how to take care of her if you don't put her down."

Reluctantly, Trent did so, but he kneeled beside her, his hand clutching hers. He didn't move when Mr. Garland returned and handed the kit to his wife. He did when Dominique turned her head to one side for the retired nurse to cleanse the wound.

With a gutteral curse, he started for the door. Neighbors hastened to get out of the way.

"Trent, please hold my hand," Dominique requested softly.

He was back in seconds, kneeling, gathering her hand in his. His were shaking. "It's going to be all right. You're going to be all right." He looked at Mrs. Garland. "Do you think we need to take her in for shock or something?"

"Just keep her warm and quiet," Mrs. Garland advised. "I don't think you'll have any trouble doing that. Mr. Scoggins is going to wait on the porch for Janice to come home."

"Here," said a middle-aged, pudgy neighbor wearing a fuzzy robe that resembled a horse blanket. She recalled his name was Mr. Carol, and that he was a history professor at the local university. "Some of my best Scotch."

Trent went to lift Dominique. An arthritic hand on his shoulder stopped him. "That's for you."

"I don't want any." Troubled, he gazed down at Dominique, and with his free hand pulled up the blanket someone had brought to cover her with to her chin. "You're warm enough? Can I get you anything?"

Now that it was over, the aftershock was getting to her. "If you're not going to drink that, I will."

Sitting her up, he let her take a sip, then another. The amber-colored drink disappeared.

A whistle of approval went up from Mr. Carol. "Now, that's a woman."

At his comment, people began talking about her subduing Isaac. His hand in hers, Trent felt her tremble. "Thank you all for helping, but I think Dominique needs to rest. Mrs. Garland, will you please see everyone out for me?"

"Of course." She lightly touched his shoulder. "You know how to contact me if you need you."

"Thank you, again," Trent said.

"You've helped us enough times," she said, then left.

No sooner had the door closed than the doorbell rang. "It's Officer Blair. I need to speak with you," called a female voice.

Trent scowled at the closed door. "If she hadn't ordered us to let those punks go, Isaac couldn't have taken a swing at you."

Dominique's fingertips touched his tense shoulder. She wanted to touch his face and crawl into his lap, but she wasn't sure of her reception. Helping her didn't mean he had forgiven her. "Isaac got the worst of it. Besides, she more than made up for it when she let you go."

His dark eyes centered on her for a long moment. The doorbell rang again.

"I don't think she's leaving," Dominique said.

Releasing her hand, Trent opened the door, then went back to sit beside Dominique and hold her hand. "The nurse said she should rest."

Officer Blair's expression didn't change at the brusque statement. She took a seat across from them and flipped open a small spiral tablet. "Of course. I just need some information for my report. Why don't we start with you, Sir?"

Trent gave the officer the information she requested, then it was Dominique's turn. She wasn't sure about the use of her assumed name, so she gave Everette as her professional name and Falcon as her legal name.

Trent tensed on hearing *Falcon*, but he didn't release her hand. Officer Blair's pen stilled, her head came up. Dominique could see realization dawning in her narrow, dark brown face.

Falcon wasn't a common name, and when Daniel Falcon hit Houston several months before, the city and state took notice. They still did.

"Any relation to Daniel Falcon?"

"My brother."

Officer Blair's eyes widened, her fingers clenched on the pen. "Sorry about the punch the kid threw at you."

"As I told Trent, you more than made up for it when you let him go." Dominique smiled. "Thank you."

The young woman's shoulders relaxed. "If you can tell me what happened, I can let you rest."

"There's not very much to tell. I was leaving here, going back home, and Isaac came from behind the shrubbery by the side of the house and grabbed me. I screamed."

Trent's hand clenched in hers.

Officer Blair frowned. "You handled yourself well. How did he get a jump on you?"

Dominique glanced at Trent. "I was thinking of something else."

"I see. That's when Mr. Masters came out?"

"Yes." This time it was Dominique who trembled.

The policewoman flipped the small notebook closed and stood. "I have all I need. An investigative officer will be assigned to the case and contact you."

"I'll be out of the studio tomorrow morning with a photo shoot," she said.

"Dominique, you're not going to work tomorrow," Trent ordered.

Calm eyes turned to him. "I beg to differ."

"I'll show myself out. Don't worry about Isaac. He finally made it to the big time with attempted kidnapping, and assault with a deadly weapon," Officer Blair told them.

"What about Jessie?" Dominique asked, remembering the frightened boy.

"He's underage, but he *was* an accessory. The court will decide." The policewoman opened the door. "By the way, you've got some nice moves."

"Thank you. My brother is an excellent teacher."

"Goodnight." The door closed after her.

Trent tucked her hand under the light blanket and pulled it to her chin. "You're sure you're warm enough?"

"Fine." *I'd be warmer if you held me, looked at me.*

"Can I get you anything?"

You. "No thanks."

He nodded, then fiddled with her covers again before his gaze locked on the small, white bandage on her neck. "I should have made sure you reached home safely."

Automatically she lifted her hand to touch his tense features, but the blanket prevented her. "You had no way of knowing Isaac would try something like that."

A muscle leaped in his jaw. "That's no excuse." His eyes finally met hers. They were filled with regret and misery. "I should have protected you better."

This time the blanket was no match for a determined woman. Trent needed her. Her hands touched his face. "You can't possibly blame yourself for Isaac's behavior. I certainly don't."

His long forefinger trembled as it lightly grazed the bandage. "He could have—" His eyes shut, his hand clenched into a tight fist.

"It's over," Dominique said, taking Trent's cold hand in hers. "I'm safe, thanks to you. If you hadn't come out, he might have succeeded in getting me into that car."

His eyes opened and they were no less haunted. "He only came after you because of me."

"Trent, stop blaming yourself." She sat up. "If it's anyone's fault, it's mine. I should have called the police the afternoon they showed up at my studio."

"What? Why didn't you tell me?" he shouted. "What afternoon?"

"The day after we slept together for the first time he and his pals came by the studio and made some crude gestures when I refused to admit them. They ran when I picked up the phone to call the police," she explained, not liking the way Trent was glaring at her.

"What stopped you from completing the call?" he asked.

She bit her lower lip. No way was she fooled by the quietness of his voice. His eyes were blazing. She had a feeling that if she weren't hurt her feet would be dangling off the floor again.

"Dominique?"

"You're not going to like it."

"I don't imagine I will, but I want to hear it, anyway."

She lay back down and drew the blanket up to her chin. "I didn't want you to get into trouble. I was safe in the studio, and I always leave before dark."

His brow furrowed. "You were trying to protect me?"

"Yes."

"I can—" he began, only to stop abruptly and stare at her, his gaze studying her more closely. "What I'm thinking can't possibly be true. You wouldn't do anything so idiotic." He pushed to his feet, took a few steps away, then quickly came back and crouched down. "You jumped Isaac when he pointed the knife at me. Why?"

She moistened her lips. This was going to be tricky. "It was the opening I had been waiting for. I wasn't going to get into that car."

'You're lying!' he shouted, pushing to his feet and glaring down at her. "You were trying to protect me again. Don't you ever take it into your head to do something like that. I can take care of myself. Do you hear me?"

She didn't think it wise to point out that the entire neighborhood could probably hear him. "Yes. Someone is at the door."

"I mean it, Dominique."

"It's probably Janice." Dominique sat up and swung her legs over the side of the sofa.

"What are you doing?" Trent asked, coming back to her.

"If Janice sees me lying down she'll think the worse. I don't want to upset her more than this is going to already," Dominique explained, reaching for the bandage.

Trent's hand stopped her. "Leave that alone."

"She'll se—"

"The bandage stays."

"Trent, be reasonable."

"Believe me, I'm giving it my best shot. Now leave that alone." Pushing to his feet, he went to answer the door. "But don't think we've finished our conversation. I still have a few things to say to you."

Dominique didn't mind the omnious threat. As long as Trent was talking to her there was a chance he might forgive her.

As soon as Trent opened the door Janice rushed inside. Paul was directly behind her. Her godmother took one look at Dominique, began fussing over her, and insisted she be taken home and put to bed. Dominique started to tell her that wasn't necessary, but Janice looked so distressed that she consented.

She had barely stood when Trent picked her up in his arms. The stubborn look in his eyes warned her to not protest.

Since she didn't know if that would be the last time she'd be held by him, be able to hold him, protesting was the furthest thing from her mind. Circling her arms around his neck, she leaned her head against his chest. Paul followed them out and closed Trent's door, while Janice rushed ahead to open her front door.

As soon as they entered Janice's house they heard the phone ringing. Dominique had expected the call. "That will be for me. Please place me on the couch by the phone."

Frowning, Trent did as she requested. "How do you know it's for you?"

"Unfortunately, from experience," she told him. Taking a deep breath, she picked up the receiver. "I'm all right Dad, Mother."

"Dominique!" Felicia cried. "We've been frantic for the past forty minutes. No one would answer the phone."

"What happened?" her practical father asked.

Dominique bit her lip and tried to think of a way to tell her parents without upsetting them, then realized that they already were. Her father's unique ability to tell when his children were deeply troubled or frightened had saved her from LaSalle, had helped Daniel out of a bad situation.

"Baby, say something?" Felicia said, her voice shaky.

"A teenager tried to make me go someplace I didn't want to," she told them. "It was over before it began."

"We're on our way," John Henry said.

"There's no need for you to come."

"There is *every* need. The helicopter Daniel sent just landed. Be safe, and know you are loved," her father said.

"Be safe, and know I love both of you, too." Her eyes misted for the first time. She hung up the phone. From her earliest memories, her father had always said good-bye to her the same way.

"You're all right?" Trent asked.

"My family is coming, and the craziness is about to begin." Her hand swept over her mussed hair. It was too late to worry about what the neighbors or the police thought. "I'd better get ready. We'll need coffee."

"And food for the hoard," Janice said.

"I'll take care of everything, Janice." Paul took her hand in his. "You just take care of Dominique."

"Thank you, Paul." She kissed his cheek.

Dominique glanced at Trent, then stood and walked toward her bedroom. There was no sense waiting. She wasn't likely to get a kiss.

Trent had never seen anything like it in his life.

Apparently, neither had Paul, because Trent had caught the amazed look on the older man's face once or twice as the evening progressed. No wonder Dominique and Janice had suggested food and drinks. He had thought they meant for her family.

Since mud had more flavor than his coffee and about the same texture, he had gladly let Paul make it. Then Paul had called his restaurant and had them deliver food. Trent never thought of leaving. He had a few things he wanted to say to Dominique.

Almost to the moment she came out of the bedroom—looking remarkably calm and breathtakingly beautiful in a white turtleneck pullover and matching pants—the door-bell had rung. Taking a seat on the Duncan Phyfe couch, she had grimaced and said, "Open the door and let the show begin."

Janice nodded. In walked the police field supervisor, who had come by to express his regret of the "unfortunate incident" and wish her well. From then on, the doorbell and the phone rang constantly.

Some of the calls were from anxious relatives, others from city or police officials who wanted to "express their regrets and drop by." She had thanked each one for calling and told them she'd be delighted to see them.

More than one official brought his wife with him. They had sipped coffee, nibbled on quiche and cherry tarts, and invited Dominique to become a member of most of the prestigious organizations in the city. Trent couldn't help but remember that Dominique Everette had not been asked.

Dominique handled them all with easy assurance, and thanked them for coming. Elegant and poised, she made a point of stating that she hoped the media did not learn what happened.

Repeatedly, she was reassured. Neither the police nor the city officials were anxious for word to circulate that a wealthy socialite had been attacked fifty feet from her home.

Janice was waving good-bye to the final guests when *they* arrived. Trent thought he had prepared himself for her brother and parents, but one look at the powerfully built men with thick hair rippling down their backs and the exquisite woman between them, and he knew he had been wrong.

They were an exotic trio. They'd stand out in any crowd, not only for their handsomeness but for their proud carriage. Here were three people who could probably spit in the devil's eye, then laugh.

He didn't know who the beautiful young pregnant woman was, or for that matter who the well-dressed elderly man was, but they definitely weren't related by blood to the Falcons or Everettes. They didn't have the coloring or the itensity.

"Mother, Dad!" Dominique cried, jumping up from the sofa and running to meet her parents. She was enveloped in a hug and rocked.

"You're sure you're all right?" Felicia asked, stepping back to look at her daughter and touching her face.

"I'm fin—" She stopped abruptly as her mother's hand slid downward and encountered the bandage.

Eyes wide, her hands shaking, Felicia slowly peeled away the collar of the turtleneck. "How bad is it? And are there any more? I want the truth."

"Just this scratch, Mother."

"Where is he?" John Henry asked, his eyes as cold as black ice.

"In jail, Dad." She smiled to soothe him. "You didn't have to fly here."

"Stop talking nonsense," Daniel said. His hand trembled as it touched her neck. His jaw clenched. "I thought I taught you better."

"If you hadn't, she would have been in a lot more trouble."

Everyone in the room turned. Trent stood in the kitchen doorway, his stance combative.

"Who are you?" Daniel asked.

"This is Trent Masters, my neighbor," Janice supplied. "Next to him is Paul Osgood. Dominique was coming from Trent's house when it happened."

Paul received no more than a cursory nod. Trent remained the center of attention. "Why didn't you see that she got home safely?" Daniel asked, his voice hard.

"At the time I thought I had good reasons." Trent's gaze was fixed on Dominique. "Now—" His hands flexed helplessly. "I'd do anything to change things."

"Trent, it wasn't your fault," Dominique cried, stepping around her parents and going to him. "Please stop blaming yourself."

"He should," John Henry said. "He should have protected you better."

Trent turned to face her family. They were all glaring at him, even the pregnant woman. Once again it struck him how little Dominique needed him. She had a family that obviously loved her very much. She certainly hadn't needed him to protect her against Isaac. If not for him, she would never have been in danger in the first place. She needed him like a fish needed a bicycle.

But he realized something. He needed her. His attention came back to her. "I'd like to talk to you alone. Will you come back to the house with me?"

"Yes," she answered without hesitation.

The vise around his heart eased. But there was still another hurdle. He turned toward Dominique's parents. She caught him by the arm. "Where are you going?"

"To ask permission. We wouldn't get two feet." This time he didn't stop until he stood in front of her unsmiling father. "Sir, you're right. I should have protected her better. My punishment is that I'll go to my grave knowing I didn't. But I'd like you to give me a second chance. I'd like your permission to speak to her privately."

"Give me one good reason why I should." John Henry asked.

"There are lots of reasons, but I'd like Dominique to hear them first," Trent told him.

"Go on, Dad, I recognize the look," Daniel said with a smile, his arm going around the pregnant woman's waist.

Trent's brow arched. He hadn't expected an ally in Daniel, nor to see his face soften as his cheek rested against the woman's head. But he was finding love had a way of changing a person and breaking all the rules. "Please, Mr. Falcon."

"If you go, Dominique, remember your promise," said the elderly man.

Trent figured the man who had spoken must be Higgins, the family friend. He was certainly outnumbered, but he wasn't giving up.

"Are you the reason she's been out every night?" Felicia asked.

"Yes, Ma'am."

"If my daughter returns upset in any way, you'll answer to me," Felicia promised.

"I want her home and safe in an hour," John Henry said flatly.

"Da—"

"Yes, Sir," Trent said, cutting Dominique off. Taking her hand, he guided her through the back kitchen door.

Trent seated Dominique on the couch in his living room. He was too nervous to sit. "Your father didn't give us much time, so I'd better get started. I'm sorry I blew up at you, and for comparing you to Margo. She had everything handed to her, and she always had her hand out, wanting more. She never worked a day in her life, never did anything during the time I knew her for someone else."

He ran his hand over his head, stopped, and stared down at Dominique. "There's no way she wouldn't have used what little influence her father had to advance herself socially. She certainly wouldn't have risked her life for me, or anyone else. You're nothing like her. Forgive me for even thinking so for a moment. You chose to make it on your own. That took courage."

"I was scared," Dominique admitted.

He sat down and took her hands. "But you didn't let that stop you. You didn't give up."

"I'm not sure what would have happened if you hadn't helped me get started."

"I might have given you the opportunity, but it was your unique ability to visualize concepts and create images that made people want you to do their portraits." He smiled proudly. "You didn't let them down. Your pictures reflect the essence of the subjects. I might have helped you get started, but you did the rest. Please say you'll forgive me."

She drew in an unsteady breath. "I do. So where do we go from here?"

"That depends on you."

"Me?"

"I'll be right back," he stated, then went down the hall into his bedroom and came back. Kneeling in front of her, he held the diamond ring between his thumb and forefinger. "I want you to have this."

Her eyes widened. She gazed from the white fire dancing in the center stone to him.

"I was going to ask you to wear it as a friendship ring."

She could barely get the words past her dry throat. *"Was? You don't want me to have it now, since you know who I am?"*

"No."

Her eyes closed in misery.

"I want you to have it because I love you, and want you to be my wife."

Her eyelids flew up. Grinning, she launched herself into his arms, almost toppling him over on the floor. Crying and kissing him, she said, "Yes. Yes. And if you ever scare me like that again I'll make you drink your own coffee for the rest of our lives together."

His arms tightened. "Dominique, I love you so much."

"You'd better, because I love you so much I ache sometimes." She held out her left hand and he slid the ring on her third finger. "It fits perfectly, just like us."

"Just like us." His eyes grew haunted. "I was so scared you wouldn't learn to love me. Then when you told me who you are, my fears escalated. You family has such a history, and so much wealth."

Her hands stroked his face. "And it doesn't mean squat if you aren't happy and don't have love. I know. Remember?"

"I only know I can't live without you. I only know that I'll love you and protect you through eternity."

"Good, because I feel the same way." Her fingers began unbuttoning his shirt.

His hands grabbed hers. "I promised to have you back in an hour."

She lifted an eyebrow. "Unless you've developed a problem I'm not aware of, that should be just enough time."

Chuckling, he picked her up in his arms and started for the bedroom. "Oh, Buttercup, I just love the way you talk."

Epilogue

The wedding announcement of Dominique Nicole Falcon and Trent Jacob Masters made headlines across the country. The media might have been caught napping and let Daniel Falcon's wedding slip past them, but they were determined to more than make up for that loss by covering every facet of his sister's engagement and nuptials.

They had a lot to cover. From the elegant announcement party at the lavish Mansion Hotel to the bridal showers held from one end of the country to the other to the hand-beaded crystal and seed pearl wedding gown to the spectacular five-foot wedding cake with blooming cascades of sugar flowers, the wedding was clearly going to be an event.

The couple was clearly in love and wanted everyone to share in their happiness. Dominique was heard saying more than once that it would be difficult for a woman *not* to fall in love with a sensitive, caring man like Trent. The

incredible thing was that somehow he had fallen in love
with her as well. The Master of Breath had blessed her
beyond belief.

Trent was not used to the spotlight, but he was comfort-
able with, and had confidence in, his future bride. On
being asked about Dominique's statement, Trent always
replied *he* was the blessed one. She was as courageous as
she was beautiful and talented. He thought it incredible
such a unique woman had fallen in love with him.

The wedding day was perfect. Sun poured from the
cloudless sky like spun gold. Barely a breeze ruffled the
yards of netting in Dominique's beaded headpiece or her
upswept hair as she rode in the open carriage with her
father. A hush fell over the church when the doors were
opened and she stood silhouetted in the light.

Always beautiful, in the ivory satin and organza gown
she appeared even more so with the glow of happiness
and love on her face. As her father led her down the aisle
strewn with rose petals in the crowded church filled with
flowers and the soft glow of candles, her twenty-five yard,
cathedral train trailed softly behind her.

Finally they reached the altar and it was time for her
father to hand her to Trent and leave. John Henry didn't
hesitate. "Be safe, and know that you are loved," he whispered, kissed her on the cheek, and stepped back.

Tears misting in her eyes, she looked at her father, her
teary-eyed and happy mother, Daniel, his arm around Madelyn, who was holding their sleeping, three week-old son,
Daniel Jr., Higgins with a lady friend, and Janice and Paul.
Love *was* possible, and infinitely preferable to being alone.

Love didn't make you vulnerable. It made you strong.

Turning, she caught sight of the stony face of her cousin,
Luke, at the end of the pew. *Your time is coming,* she thought.
Smiling, she blinked back tears and reached her gloved

hand out to Trent, who stood tall and proud. His hand closed securely around hers.

I love you, he mouthed.

I love you, she returned.

Slouched in his seat, Luke barely kept a grimace off his face.

He had yet to learn about love, but he would.

In time.

Dear Readers:

Thanks goes out to you and the booksellers once again for putting another of my books, SILKEN BETRAYAL, on *Blackboard,* the African-American national best-selling list at #3. The list was reprinted in the January 98 issue of *Essence* magazine. Your continued support means so very much to me.

The snail mail and email on **HEART OF THE FALCON** was fantastic. I really appreciate all of you and your comments. Many asked about Madelyn's brothers, Kane and Matt. Kane and Victoria's story is **FOREVER YOURS,** and Matt and Shannon's is **ONLY HERS.** Sorry, I failed to include the titles in my last letter.

Hope you enjoyed getting to know Dominique and Trent. For those of you who think I might have forgotten Trent's mother, don't despair. I have a surprise or two in store for him. First, there is another matter that needs my immediate attention. I feel a headache coming on already.

Take care and all the best,

Francis Ray
Francis Ray

Francis Ray
P.O. Box 764423
Dallas, Texas 75376

Web site: http://www.tlt.com/authors/fray.htm

LOOK FOR THESE ARABESQUE ROMANCES